FINDING THE SUUN

LEGENDS OF THE FALLEN BOOK 6

J. A. CULICAN

CASSIDY TAYLOR

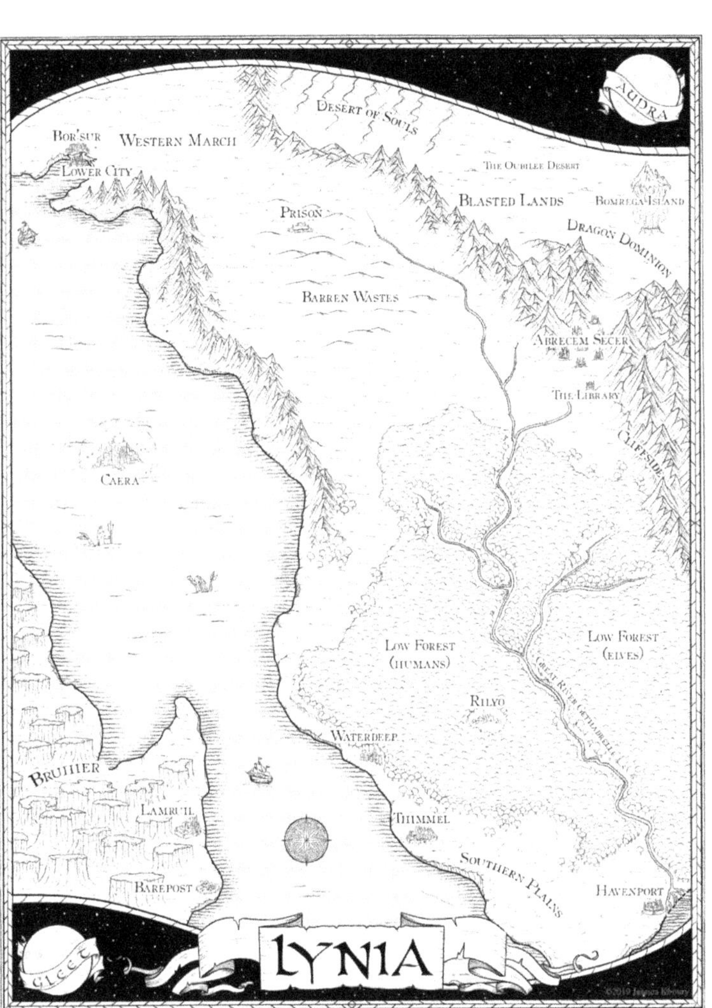

AUDRA
GLCCC
LYNIA
DESERT OF SOULS
BOR'SUR
WESTERN MARCH
LOWER CITY
THE OUBILEE DESERT
PRISON
BLASTED LANDS
BOMREGA ISLAND
DRAGON DOMINION
BARREN WASTES
ABRECEM SECER
THE LIBRARY
CLIFFSIDE
CAERA
LOW FOREST
(HUMANS)
LOW FOREST
(ELVES)
RILYO
GREAT RIVER CETILADREEL
WATERDEEP
BRUHIER
LAMRUIL
THIMMEL
SOUTHERN PLAINS
HAVENPORT
BAREPOST
©2019 Inkpots Library

CHAPTER 1

"You are not welcome here."

The harsh words came from a humorless man who also happened to be the High Elven king. Bruhier wasn't a monarchy, but the elves did what they wanted. He was the elven representative for the governing co-op, and if they wanted to call him their king, who would tell them no?

"You must leave." His cold blue eyes surveyed our group, which consisted of me, my elder brother Erik, my elder sister Estrid, our griffin friend Stiarna, and Arun, High Elf turned adventurer. I knew we had to look rough, having just spent what felt like days fighting off ur'gels and trying not to drop out of the sky. "Immediately."

We'd come straight here from the docks, led by Captain Wynleth who had made herself scarce since delivering us to the throne room. The king had not heard our story or entertained our pleas for assistance. He hadn't even let us speak, not even Arun, who was one of his own.

Erik, our usual spokesperson, cleared his throat. "Your Highness, we've been through so much. All we ask for—"

"What you ask is insignificant to me and my people. What *is* significant is that you brought danger to Lamruil. A type of danger that the elven people have not seen for generations."

Erik tried again. "But—"

"You are not allowed in Lamruil. By order of the king, you are to return to your ship and take your leave of our fine city."

Well, there was *truly little* that made me more upset than being ignored or ordered around, and this guy was doing both.

I raised my hand and stepped forward. "If I may?"

Arun clapped a hand on my shoulder and tried to drag me back in line, but I shook him off and moved out of his reach, never taking my eyes off the elf in front of me. He might have been Arun's king, but he wasn't mine.

"No, you may not."

"Well, then I will anyway."

Erik reached for me next. "Come on, Frida. Let's not stay where we're not welcome."

But I stepped away from him too, moving closer to where the king stood on his raised dais. The guards in their red jackets converged in front of the king, swords crossed so I could get no closer.

I held my hands up to show I was harmless, though I wasn't really. But they didn't need to know that. "This danger is coming whether we're here or not. War is coming to all the lands of Iynia, and not even the Bruish High Elves are immune here in your towers."

One of the king's advisors, a squirrel-faced man who stood to his right, scoffed. "You should not speak so to the king. Guards."

The two guards moved to grab me, but the king stopped them with a flick of his fingers. I didn't know how they could have even seen the small movement.

The king looked down his nose at me. It was a look that would have cowed anyone else, but I was done being bossed around. "How can you know this?"

"I've seen things you can only imagine. I've met the dreamwalker who freed Beru Halsted from the prison in the Barren Wastes."

At Beru's name, a wave of noise crashed through the room as the gentry elves lining the walls turned to each other. I knew some of them wouldn't know his name, but those who did would fill everyone else in. Elves had exceptionally long lives, and some of them might have even known him when he served Onen Suun before his accidental imprisonment.

"When she did, it caused a crack in the magic that held Dag'-draath in the prison," I continued before I could lose their attention. "His minions are fleeing the prison—including the ur'gels that you saw today."

The king's advisor scoffed rudely. "Impossible. Lies. The ur'gels are confined to the Blasted Lands."

I could tell the king believed me. Maybe he was their king for a reason. He ignored his advisor. "What did they want with you?"

That had me stumped. If I told him they were after me, we'd be right back where we started.

While I scrambled for words, Arun came forward, his head bowed. "We know how to find the key to the prison, and the ur'gels know that. They're trying to stop us, but we might be the only ones who can stop them. And Dag'draath."

It wasn't exactly the whole truth, but it wasn't a lie either.

I felt bolstered by Arun's support. "You cannot hide from this, Your Highness. Another Dark War is coming, and you have the chance right now to help us stop it."

The king stroked his long grey beard with two fingers. "Unless your key is here on Lamruil, then I would say the same to you. Hiding here will not further your mission, but it will endanger my people."

"We only ask for a few days to rest and recover supplies."

"And make repairs to the ship," Arun added.

The king shifted his icy gaze to Arun. I wondered if he recognized him as a member of the Phina family, or if any of the elves in the throne room were kin to Arun. Had he been gone so long that no one knew him? Surely Tsarra Trisfina would, but she was also nowhere to be seen. "How long?"

Arun wrung his hands together in front of him, his eyes on the king's feet. They were nice feet, clothed in shiny leather boots, but certainly not worthy of such attention. "A week at least, two at most."

"Too long," the king declared without hesitation. "We do not have the power to defend Lamruil against ur'gel attacks for that much time."

Arun looked apologetic as he said, "There is no other option. The *Duchess* will hardly get us off the plateau in her current condition."

"No other option?" The king actually smiled, and it was more fearful than his grimace. "You dare tell a king that there is no other option?" Then, to his advisor, "Bring me Captain Wynleth."

A few moments of strained silence passed before the doors at the back of the hall banged open and the captain who had retrieved us from the air docks stalked down the aisle with long, purposeful strides. She pushed past, ignoring us, and dropped to a knee in front of the guards, removing her hat from her head. Her curly black hair, formerly tamed by the tricorn hat, practically exploded around her head.

The king flicked his hand at her in an upward motion. "Rise, Captain Wynleth."

She did, pressing the hat to her chest. I saw that she'd been stripped of her weapons, her belts empty. I would have bet my life on the fact that they'd missed one or two, stashed in a boot or a thigh holster. "How can I be of service, Your Highness?"

"These folks require passage on an incredibly special mission, one of the utmost importance. You've been itching to leave Lamruil. Here is your chance." The king motioned to us, and the captain turned her eyes on me. They were a brown so light they were practically gold, and they offered me no kindness at all. Then her gaze shifted to Arun and something like recognition flickered there before the mask of indifference slammed back down.

She obviously wanted to ask questions, but she pressed her lips together until their edges turned white. "Yes, Your Highness."

"You will leave in the morning. Get them what supplies they need and depart before sunrise."

"As you wish, Your Highness."

The king wasted no time dismissing us. We scampered back down the aisle, the captain at our heels. I was glad when we emerged into the fresh air, but my relief was short-lived.

When the doors shut behind us, Arun turned on her. "I do not need your ship, Captain."

Captain Wynleth replaced the hat on her head, pressing down on it firmly. "I'm afraid you do." Then she turned to Erik, ignoring Arun, which I thought exceptionally rude. "I trust you can find your own accommodations for the night. I will meet you at sunrise onboard."

"What is the ship's name?" Erik asked.

A guard approached the captain and handed her a bundle of weapons. She took them from him and strapped them on meticulously, knowing exactly where each blade went. Finally, she deigned to answer Erik. "The *Wind Wraith*." With those final words, Captain Wynleth tipped her hat at my brother and stalked away, leaving us on the palace steps.

Arun was in a foul mood as he led us down the main street to a three-story inn he said he knew from before, when he'd lived in his family's estate on the edge of town. He barely spoke, and when he did, he gave short, one-word answers.

When we reached the inn's doors, he turned to Stiarna. "You can't come in."

She eyed him unblinkingly before turning and slinking away into the shadows of the street.

Arun rented two rooms—one for him and Erik, and another for me and Estrid. After a late dinner, begrudgingly served by an elven innkeeper who scowled the whole time, Erik and Estrid joined a card game in the tavern against Arun's advice.

Not one for cards, I retired to my room, where I washed as best as I could in the wash basin and threw open the shutters to absorb what I could of the city before we had to leave. My eyes took in the gold and glass towers, the shining streets lit by yooperlite lanterns, the sprawling estates that seemed to climb the plateau's sides. And then, as they always did, my eyes found the night sky. The stars were barely visible beyond the lights of the city, but a few bright ones were winking at me slyly.

I leaned my chin on my hands and sighed, and when I did, a voice came from the window beside me. "Frida?"

"Arun?" I stood and peeked outside, my hands on the windowsill to brace myself as I twisted to try to see him. He was doing the same thing. "What are you doing?"

"Same thing you're doing, I expect."

"Looking at the stars and thinking about your mother?"

He smiled but it wasn't a happy smile. "More like my sister." He'd told me about her, his sister who had died as a young girl, his first lost cause. "Come out with me."

I withdrew and looked down at myself. I was dressed in my shift and my hair was slicked back with water. But I didn't get a chance to say no, because Arun appeared at my window, crouching on the small overhang that protruded below our windows. It was barely wide enough for him to fit.

"Don't leave me out here alone." He held his hand out to me.

What choice did I really have? I let him take my hand and lead me outside, where I sat beside him, my back to the window, my legs dangling over the street below. I was acutely aware of how close we were to each other, one entire side of my body alight with the warmth of his. After a few moments of comfortable silence, he pointed to a cluster of lights farther down the ridge, near the very edge of the plateau.

"That's the Phina estate," he said.

It was difficult to see in the dark, but I saw the shape of a sprawling multilevel home and what I expected were acres and acres of land. I couldn't imagine coming home and not seeing my family, especially if our home looked like that. "Why didn't we stay there?"

He shrugged, and I felt it more than saw it. "I'm afraid that if I go there, I won't ever leave again."

I grunted. "I'm the opposite, afraid I won't ever be able to find my way home again."

After that, we didn't talk about much of significance, but every little thing I learned about him felt important. He pointed out the school he'd attended as a child, and his best friend's small townhouse just down the main road from the inn. He told me about parties on the estate and how he would always escape and sit in the barn's loft, usually alone but sometimes with girls.

"So, you take all the girls out on roofs?" I asked, playfully knocking my shoulder into his.

He shook his head and didn't turn to look at me when he spoke. "You're the only girl I've wanted to take out on the roof since I first saw you in the mine."

"Arun …," I started, but I didn't know what I wanted to say. Did I want to discourage him and try to protect myself from the moment he left me? Or did I want to take advantage of it now and enjoy his attentions while I could? I knew what my siblings would say, each of them something different, but what did I want?

Before I could respond, though, Arun smiled at me, showing off dazzling white teeth. "Can we just forget I said that?"

Without missing a beat, I nodded and launched into the story of when my father gave me my ax when I turned thirteen and I had very nearly shaved half of Estrid's head. She liked that look so much that she'd kept it that way for the last seven years.

Arun laughed joyfully, a sound I hadn't heard much of since before the attack on Lunla's temple. When his laughter died down, he put his hand on my leg, almost as an afterthought. For the first time, my reaction wasn't to pull away, but to take his hand in mine and not let go.

Dawn came too soon. I'd crept back into my room a few hours before sunrise when I'd barely been able to keep my eyes open. Estrid had already been in the bed, snoring loudly, and I'd fallen in it beside her, sleep taking me immediately. Erik banged on our door what felt like moments later. We'd risen, dressed, and met Erik and Arun downstairs in the tavern, where they were arguing with the innkeeper about the price of supplies.

"That's thievery," Arun said.

The innkeeper said something rude in return but I missed it, busy as I was taking in the sight of him with new eyes after last night. There was what I'd always known. He was big—not as big as Erik, but still tall and wide with heavily muscled arms. He had shaggy, dark hair, longer than mine, that he sometimes wore loose, but was now pulled back out of his face in a messy knot, exposing his pointed ears.

But there were also the subtle things I'd never really noticed before. The dimple in his cheek when he frowned. The way he shifted from foot to foot as he argued with the innkeeper, unable to ever be completely still. The way he seemed to unconsciously search for me every now and then, and smile when his eyes met mine. It was surprising how suddenly he'd become a part of our group, when it had been just the three of us for so long. More than that, he was someone I could adventure with, someone who wouldn't make me settle down. Someone who would see the world with me rather than keep it from me.

Arun scooted down the bar to where I stood, unaware of the scrutiny he'd been under. "Here," he said, offering me a round brass box on a long chain.

I took it, my eyebrows drawing together in confusion. "What's this for?"

He had me hold it flat in my palm and twisted a small latch. It popped open to reveal a compass. "I had the innkeeper throw it in with everything else. I thought... Well, the stone wasn't working, but I thought maybe this would remind you can always find your way home, or wherever it is you want to go."

The stone. I hated the thought of it. Ravyn, the priest from the Valley of the Horses, had given it to me and told me it would guide me to the Suun heir. But when I'd taken it out in our moment of need, it had done nothing, given me no signal. I didn't even know what to tell the stern Captain Wynleth when we boarded her ship in a few minutes. *Oh, just fly around until the rock tells us to turn.* I had a feeling she would drop me off under the veil so fast my head would spin.

Instead of thinking about that, I studied the compass, running my finger over the glass cover, examining the worn artistry of the background. When I looked up, I realized that the black-tipped needle was pointing directly at him. "Thank you."

"I know it's kind of weird, but I saw it and I thought of you and ... what we talked about last night."

"It's not weird." To prove my point, I slipped the chain over my neck and dropped the compass inside my shirt.

The innkeeper reappeared then with Erik and Estrid on his heels, both of them carrying large bags of supplies—food, clothes, and even a couple stones of yooperlite. Arun took the one from Estrid, thanking the innkeeper.

The sky was just lightening when we emerged onto the street and hurried in the direction of the docks. Stiarna was already there, waiting for us at the door. She fell in line beside me.

"What are you going to do with the *Duchess*?" I asked Arun, reaching over to scratch Stiarna's shoulder.

He shifted the bag to another shoulder, and we crossed the street. "I've already sent word to the estate. Our coachman will retrieve her and hire someone to do the repairs."

"Your coachman." I nodded. "Sure."

Captain Wynleth was waiting for us on the dock beside her ship, which looked very much like the *Duchess*, with its three masts and a dozen sails, but more polished. It had definitely not seen as much action as Arun's ship, or if it had, she'd been here long enough to do extensive repairs. I almost felt bad for what I knew she was about to face.

Almost.

Even less when I saw her look Arun up and down before speaking. "I thought I would have to send the guards after you."

Arun looked to the east. "We have plenty of time left." He was being generous. The sun had very nearly risen over the city, which had become practically blinding with the sunlight reflecting off the glass buildings.

We followed her on board. Her crew lined up to meet us, or her, rather. She barked orders at most of them, but one held back. He was short and skinny, with close-cropped yellow hair and pointed ears decorated with golden wire. "This is Renwick, my first mate."

Renwick nodded at us but didn't speak.

Erik introduced each of us in turn, Arun last.

"Phina," Captain Wynleth said, looking down her nose at her fellow elf. "I thought you looked familiar."

Arun narrowed his eyes at her but shook his head. "I'm afraid you have me at a disadvantage."

"And I plan to keep it that way." She dismissed us with a wave of her hand. When she walked away, she held her hands clasped behind her back, which was as straight as an arrow.

We followed Renwick to our quarters, where we were all crammed into one room.

As we claimed our cots, I turned to Arun. "Captain Wynleth really hates you. What did you do to her?"

He sat on one of the cots and it swung beneath him. "Does it make me a horrible person to admit that I have no idea?"

"Yes," Estrid said. "Definitely."

We returned to the deck at Renwick's urging, where we were met with organized chaos. Unlike when Arun had ordered us around, this crew knew what they were doing.

Wynleth stood at the helm and turned to us. "There are only two rules that you need to know in order to fly on my ship. First, I am the captain, and my word is the law. If I tell you to do something, you do it." Then, focusing on Arun, she said, "And second, no one touches the ship's wheel except for me and Renwick."

"I have experience," Arun said. "I can help."

She blinked at him, and then turned to me. "What was the rule again?"

I couldn't help but smile when I answered. "No one touches the ship's wheel."

Arun glared at her. "But I am a ship's captain. I will not be treated as a common passenger."

Wynleth looked him over again. "Captain of a stolen ship is no captain at all." Then she adjusted her tricorn, tilting it at a cocky angle that made me think I could actually come to like her. "Besides, what kind of captain doesn't have a hat?"

"I don't need—"

But she was done, returning to the helm and leaving us to

Renwick. He set us to menial chores, carrying buckets of water and hanging onto ropes while more accomplished sailors tied the knots. Finally, the *Wind Wraith* pulled out of its slip and angled away from the city.

From her spot at the helm, Wynleth called to us. "Where to?"

It was the moment I'd been dreading. I pulled the rock from my vest and held it flat in my palm. Erik, Estrid, and Arun looked down at it with me.

"Still nothing?" Estrid asked.

Renwick poked his head over my shoulder. "That looks like a wayfinder's stone."

We all turned to look at him.

"A what?"

"A wayfinder's stone," he repeated as if that would clear things up for us. He patted his pockets, looking for something. "An old sailor's trick. You just need a compass."

I looked up at Arun, surprised.

He smiled and raised his eyebrows at me as if he'd known this would happen all along.

"I have one." I pulled the compass out from my shirt and flipped it open. "Now what?"

Renwick put the four-pointed stone flat in my right hand, the compass in the other. Then he turned me by the shoulders so that I was facing north. Almost immediately, the rock grew warm and began to glow faintly in the spot on it that corresponded with east on the compass. I looked up at Renwick, exhaling with relief.

"Is it working?" he asked.

I nodded, too delighted to speak.

"It was created for you, so it will only work for you. You'll have to work closely with the captain on our journey."

"East," I told him. "Toward the coast."

Renwick left to deliver the heading to Captain Wynleth, and we were on our way, finally, to find the Suun heir.

CHAPTER 3

While the others dispersed to complete whatever menial task Renwick set them to do, I stood on the deck, the compass and the stone in my hands to confirm the heading. It kept us pointing east, and I began to trust Ravyn a little more. I felt hopeful for the first time since starting this crazy chase.

But then the compass began to shift, and I realized Wynleth was changing course. In the distance, a small island that looked like part of Lamruil's outer rim came into view. And it seemed that we were headed straight toward it.

I stood below the helm and called up to her. "We're off course."

She looked down at me, her eyes narrowed in a way that struck me as particularly cruel. "No, we're not."

"Yes, we are." I held up the compass as proof.

"I am the captain of the *Wind Wraith*, and she goes where I tell her, and it is always intentional."

"Then why are we going *there*?" I pointed at the small plateau, an island in a sea of clouds. It was much smaller than Lamruil, and much more crowded. The houses were not sprawling estates but packed in tightly in the small space. There were only a few flying ships docked at small, personal piers that jutted out over the southern edge of the plateau.

"There's a stop we have to make before we continue on your quest."

I wanted to keep arguing with her. To tell her that we hadn't agreed to this and that I did not, in fact, have time for any side trips. But I knew with certainty that she wouldn't entertain any objections. That they would likely have the opposite effect and make her even more determined to make this little detour.

Instead, I went and told on her. Erik and Arun were helping two other men do something with a sail. "She's stopping."

Arun stood and looked around. When he spotted the island, he froze. "Is that Fairlow?"

"I wouldn't know."

He muttered a curse that left Erik and me exchanging a confused glance, and abandoned his post, stalking toward the helm.

When Captain Wynleth saw him, she smiled. "Can I help you, Phina?"

"What are we doing at Fairlow?"

"There's someone there I thought we should stop and say hello to."

I turned to Arun. "What is she talking about?"

He ignored me. "That wasn't part of our deal."

"Our deal?" She scoffed at him. "I'm transporting you and the D'ahvol only because my high king ordered me to. I will take her where she needs to go, but I made you no promises about where else our journey might take us."

Arun swung himself up on the helm and glared at her, nose-to-nose. "What do you want from me? Who are you?"

Captain Wynleth raised an eyebrow. "Figured it out, have you?"

"Not really," Arun answered. "Only that you have some

personal vendetta against me, and you'll make the whole quest suffer for it."

I didn't know what they were talking about, but I had never seen Arun like this. Usually the peacemaker who put an end to confrontations, something about the sight of this place had him very irritated.

"Is it because of her?" Captain Wynleth jerked her chin at me, bringing me into an argument I had no part in.

Arun considered me over his shoulder. "No," he finally answered. "It's not."

"Then why?" she hissed at him. "Why have you betrayed my cousin this way?"

"Your ... your what?" Arun stuttered.

"Who?" I asked, looking between the two of them.

Instead of explaining, Arun looked the captain up and down. Then, he asked, "Tsarra is your cousin?"

Realizing that she'd revealed too much, she looked away, eyes focused once more on our trajectory. "Her mother is my mother's sister."

"So, you know about—"

"The betrothal? Yes. Your betrayal? Also, that."

Now that he knew what was happening, Arun seemed a little calmer. "Even if she is your cousin, I don't see what that has to do with you."

"She is family." Then, looking down her nose at him, "I know family has never meant much to you."

The semblance of calm that had come over him dissipated and his cheeks flushed red with what I assumed was fury. She couldn't have known about the death of his sister, or she never would have said that. Everything he'd done was because of the love he'd had for her, the love that hadn't had anywhere to go after her death. The fact that I knew that, and she didn't bolstered me slightly.

In an attempt to split them up, I stepped forward. "What does any of this have to do with this place? With Fairlow?"

Arun was the one who answered. "Tsarra's father was on the high king's council. When he made an exceptionally unwise decision, it cost him his title and his estate. He was banished to Fairlow."

"Why here?"

"Because Fairlow is the epicenter of the slave trade for Lamruil. He's been reduced to managing the auctions, while his family is charged with caring for the slaves during their time here. Truly, they are little better than servants for the merchant and gentry classes."

I hated the idea of slavery. Thankfully, the D'ahvol were too brutal to be victims of the elves, but humans were not so lucky. But I wasn't here to argue the merits of enslaving a people just because elves thought of themselves as superior. "And marrying you …"

"Marrying *any* High Elf would give the family credibility and return them to their place in court. Her father might never be on the council again, but his honor would be restored."

Elven politics made me sick to my stomach. A D'ahvol would have just killed him and been done with it, but this game of secret movements and underhanded betrothals was worse.

Arun turned back to the captain. "If you know Tsarra, you know that she and I aren't suited for each other. It was a match of convenience. Her father wanted her to marry to regain his position. My mother wanted me to settle down and stay home."

All that might have been true, but there was one thing he was forgetting. "But she came for you."

Captain Wynleth pointed at me as if we were suddenly on the same side. "That's right. She came for you when you were taken by that human governor."

"It was just an attempt to protect her family." He looked over his shoulder at the island that was growing closer. "The marriage was a bad idea."

"Then why did you agree to it?" I asked, feeling suddenly sick to my stomach.

He turned toward me completely, his back to the captain, who once again looked satisfied at my question. I didn't like giving her any ammunition, but they were questions I needed the answer to before I let him in any further.

"When I agreed to it, I didn't have any reason not to. The Trisfina family was another lost cause that I was going to try to fix. Now ..."

"Now?"

He didn't meet my eyes as he said, "Now, I think I might have a reason to say no."

Was I that reason? Or was it something else? The mission, maybe, to save the world from a second Dark War. To find the heir and guide her on her path to the light. I didn't know which one I wanted it to be. I didn't know which one the bigger lost cause was.

Wynleth wasn't having it, though. "Well, then you'll have to say no to her face. Only then will I take the D'ahvol where her stone wants us to go."

Arun looked between the two of us, but I didn't say anything to sway his decision one way or the other. If she dropped me and my siblings in the middle of a Bruhier valley, we would find a way to survive and make our way to where we were supposed to go. It would be harder than just flying there, but we would find our way with or without her. We always had.

"Fine," he finally answered, but he didn't have much of a choice. The *Wind Wraith* was already pulling into a rickety-looking slip at the edge of an even worse-looking market. The half-empty stalls were covered with dingy white cloths, and the streets were practically empty.

After instructing Stiarna to stay put lest she scare the locals, we disembarked. A man stepped out of the dock house and moved down the pier toward us, a younger boy on his heels. Arun hung back and I suspected that this was Mr. Trisfina. It wasn't just Arun's hesitancy but also the man's appearance. His grey hair was thin, falling around his pointed ears, and his jacket, once fine, was threadbare and conspicuously missing the button that would keep it closed across his belly.

"May I help—" He stopped, drawing up short when he saw Captain Wynleth stalking toward him with her usual long strides. "Quynn?"

"Uncle." She grasped him around the wrist in greeting and he pulled her close.

The boy behind him whispered something to Mr. Trisfina, who snapped back, "No, we will not charge them." The boy shut his ledger and scurried away back to the dock house. Then, to Quynn, "What brings you to Fairlow? Are you here for the … auction?" His eyes skimmed over the rest of us, not finding any of us in chains.

"No, Uncle. I've brought someone who needs to speak to you and Tsarra." Quynn dragged Arun forward.

It took a few moments for recognition to register in the old man's eyes. "Phina," he breathed. "You've come for Tsarra at last? I thought—we thought—"

Arun grimaced. "No, Lord Trisfina."

"What am I lord of, exactly?" Mr. Trisfina laughed humorlessly and held his arms out to the side. "I am no lord, not anymore. Please, call me Laurel." Then, he put his arm around Arun's shoulder, eyeing me and my siblings over his shoulder. "Come, let us speak in private."

Arun and Mr. Trisfina disappeared into the dock house, while Captain Wynleth stalked away without another word to us.

"Shall we explore a bit?" Estrid asked. "Stretch our land-legs before getting back on the ship?"

Erik and I agreed, and the three of us moved through the market, drawing open stares from the elves gathered around the stalls. I guessed it wasn't common to see outsiders coming to Fairlow of their own volition, unless they were here to buy slaves. Our D'ahvol heritage would give us away in that—we did not keep slaves or condone the practice. Maybe they feared we were here to start trouble. Well, I wouldn't say no to a good fight.

Estrid stopped to buy three bright red apples from a vendor, and then we waited around while a smithy polished all our weapons for just one coin each. He ground my ax against the whetstone with expert precision that not even I could match. When he returned it to me, just a touch with the tip of my finger brought blood welling to the surface through a small cut. I gave him an extra coin just for that, and then hurried to catch up with Erik and Estrid who had already rounded a corner up ahead.

They were easy to catch, though, because they'd come to a stop at the edge of a large crowd.

The market had been mostly empty, and now I knew why. "Looks like we found all the people," I said.

"What is this?" Erik asked, mostly to himself.

Estrid tapped a man on the shoulder. "What's going on?"

He turned around, already looking annoyed, but when he took in the sight of us with our freshly polished weapons, he took a step back, knocking into the elf in front of him. "The auction."

The *slave* auction, I surmised. "Come on, I don't want to see this." I tugged on Estrid's sleeve, but Erik was already moving forward, cutting through the crowd. No one protested. In fact, most of them moved aside to let him pass, so Estrid and I hurried behind him in his wake. It wasn't until we were to the front and I could move aside and see the auction block that I saw what had him so worked up.

Standing there, on the raised auction block in a brown muslin dress, was Aysche Luthair, Governor Luthair's niece and all-around terrible bitch. My hand covered my mouth in shock. She looked even worse than she had the last time I'd seen her, after the fight with the ur'gels, when she had cursed me as I'd walked away. What had happened to her since then? She was skinny, her curvy figure reduced to bones, and her hair was dark and stringy with grease. To make it worse, she was looking down at her feet, without a spark of her former defiant attitude. I hated Aysche, that was true, but no one deserved to be sold into slavery, not even her.

Before I could even decide whether or not to try to do anything about it though, Erik had rushed forward in true Frida fashion, swords blazing. The man I assumed was the auctioneer opened his mouth to object, but Erik had his blade to his throat before he could get a sound out. The rest of the crowd was frozen.

So was I, shocked into stillness, but Estrid was not. She rushed forward, cutting Aysche's bonds with her knife.

"This woman is not a slave," Erik announced. "Where did you get her?"

The auctioneer stuttered, waving a document in the air. Erik snatched it, read it, then crumpled it into a ball and shoved it into one of his pockets.

Estrid had already freed Aysche, but the girl wasn't moving. There was a commotion to my left and I saw a platoon of red-coated guards trying to shove their way through the gathered crowd.

"Come on," I hissed. "Now." I could only hope that Arun was done with Mr. Trisfina and ready to beat a hasty retreat.

Estrid took a step forward but Aysche didn't move. She didn't even look up, or object, or throw any rude remarks at us. She was a shell of her former self.

Erik saw and tossed the auctioneer aside. The blundering

man scrambled for his spectacles, which had fallen into the dirt somewhere below the dais. Then my brother put his shoulder to Aysche's waist and lifted her over his shoulder. The Aysche I'd known in Barepost would have never let him do it, but this Aysche just hung there limply as he jumped down from the dais and joined us.

This time, Estrid led us through the crowd. No one tried to stop us. I wondered what they were thinking. Probably that we were kidnapping her, being that we were savage D'ahvol and all.

I heard the auctioneer yelling something at the guards, his voice high with panic. "Faster," I urged, putting my hands on Estrid's back.

We were through the crowd and rushing down the market street when I spotted Arun admiring silver baubles at one of the stalls. I shouted for him to go, grabbing his shoulder as we passed and dragging him along.

"What in Onen's name?" He looked back, confused, then his eyes widened. I didn't want to know what he saw behind us.

"I'll explain when we're on the ship," I said breathlessly.

"That seems like it would be best."

We were already down the pier before Mr. Trisfina's scribe emerged from the dock house, shouting for us to stop. His shouts were quickly swallowed by the pounding steps of the guards in pursuit. Luckily, Captain Wynleth seemed to have seen us and was already preparing the *Wind Wraith* for departure.

On board, my sister and I drew in the gangplank while Erik and Arun dropped Aysche to the deck. We pulled out of the slip almost immediately, the sails filling with wind as Wynleth shouted orders at her crew. She was no longer the hurt, angry cousin, but had become once again the captain of her ship.

It wasn't until we were well out of sight of Fairlow that she turned the wheel over to Renwick and came down to stand over us, arms crossed and face grim. "I do believe that you owe me an explanation. I know you do not understand the ways of the elves, but that doesn't give you the right to steal from us just because you disagree with our practices."

Erik pulled the slip of paper from his pocket and handed it up to her. "You're telling me that the elves condone dealing in kidnapped humans?"

I sidled up beside Wynleth and looked over her shoulder. It was a bill of sale, with Aysche's name listed as "Unknown Luthair." Her seller was listed as "Unknown Dragon." There was a note scrawled below indicating that she'd been captured in the valley below Barepost and that she claimed to be the governor's niece, although her appearance would suggest otherwise. She had looked awful after the fight with the ur'gels, nothing like the little princess she always pretended to be. And the dragons did have an ongoing conflict with Governor Luthair, ever since they'd ruined one of his trading ships and he'd captured one of their own, enslaving it in the mines. Arun had freed that dragon, but then Luthair's men had killed the dragons who were left guarding the *Iron Duchess* on top of the plateau. Now the dragons had stolen the governor's niece from her home. It was a never-ending circle of revenge.

"This woman is the niece of Governor Luthair of Barepost," Estrid explained from her place at the captain's other shoulder.

Captain Wynleth balled the paper in her fist. "Perhaps he sold her to the dragons."

I cocked a disbelieving eyebrow at her. "He would never do that," I said, surprised that I was defending him, but absolutely certain in my conviction. He was conniving and cruel, but he would never have allowed a legitimate Luthair to be sold into slavery.

"My uncle will have to answer to the guards," she said, her forehead wrinkled with frown lines as she stared down at Aysche. "He let us land."

I pulled out the compass and the rock and held them

together, waiting for direction. It once again pointed us to the east. "Did you tell him where we were going?"

She shook her head. "Only that we were headed east."

"Maybe we should go south for a while to throw them off."

Captain Wynleth's cocky smile returned. "They'll never catch the *Wind Wraith*." She returned to her place at the helm, barking something at Renwick who slinked away.

Erik was trying to coax fresh water down Aysche's throat. She had enough of her wits about her to turn her head away, refusing the water and instead letting it dribble down her chin, but she still didn't speak. Stiarna nibbled at Aysche's loose hair but got no reaction from the girl and abandoned her, returning to her spot at the bow of the ship.

Arun was standing nearby, staring down at them, his brow furrowed. His eyes were distant though, somewhere far away, but when he felt me looking at him, he snapped back to the present moment, looking from me to Erik, then to Estrid on his other side. "There's something else."

"Something else? What do you mean?" I shoved my hand through my hair, bracing myself for whatever else could possibly be happening.

"Lord—Mr. Trisfina told me that Tsarra had returned to Fairlow but left again not long ago, and he doesn't know where she went."

"Okay...," I said slowly.

"She left with, as Mr. Trisfina put it, 'a human woman with golden hair and a smile that made him want to kill someone.'"

I groaned and turned away from the group. The fall from the airship hadn't killed her, then. I should have put my ax through her heart.

Erik sighed, not looking up. "Savarah."

The name sent a shiver down my spine. I definitely didn't like the reverent way Erik said it. He'd turned her away once, but I didn't know if he would be able to do it again.

Estrid was the one to wonder aloud, "What is she up to now?"

Unfortunately, none of us had any answers.

All we could do was continue on our way and wait for her to show herself.

CHAPTER 4

We flew east all afternoon and did not come across another plateau peeking above the veil. I was glad for it, not sure if I would be ready to face whatever waited for us at our destination, especially if it had to do with Savarah. She'd been a thorn in my side since my friend Harbin had brought her to me. I wondered now if he'd been under her influence when he'd done so, and if he ever would have otherwise. A part of me regretted ever accepting her mission to free Arun, but another part of me knew if I hadn't, I never would have met the elf or left Barepost.

Captain Wynleth checked in with me regularly, but the wayfinder's stone did not change, guiding us ever eastward. The clouds rolled below us, thick and impenetrable, a sea of white and grey. The sun chased us until finally letting us go, dipping below the veil, and plunging our world into darkness. The crew of the *Wind Wraith* ran along the railing, activating the yooperlite lanterns on the posts until we were in our own circle of dull yellow light.

It seemed like it was only at night, when everyone else was sleeping, that Arun and I were able to find time to talk. I hadn't seen him the rest of the afternoon, so I went looking for him after my siblings had retired to our cabin, taking Aysche, who was still practically catatonic, with them.

I found him at the helm, talking to the captain. Neither of them heard me approach from below, and it wasn't until I was close that I realized exactly how near to each other the two of them were standing.

Arun was leaning against the railing beside the wheel, his face just inches from hers. "So, that's why you hate me, then? Because of the issue with Trisfina?"

The captain did not move away from him. Instead, she looked him right in the eyes. "No."

"There's something else?" Arun smiled, and I didn't like the way he said it. Like there was another meaning to his words, one that I would never understand.

"There's always something else," she confirmed, smiling back at him. It wasn't a kind smile, or a mean one. But ... something else.

"I don't think you really hate me at all." Arun leaned away, crossing his arms over his broad chest. "I think you admire me."

She looked away from him finally, trying and failing to suppress a smile. "You're crazy."

But I didn't think he was. I thought she maybe more than admired him, in spite of the fact they were constantly at each other's throats. And it made sense. They were from the same world. A world that had no place for someone like me.

Feeling silly for ever thinking it was anything more than a companionship of necessity with Arun, I slunk away without being seen.

Below deck, I fell into the cot above Aysche, determined to only wallow in self-pity until the sun rose. My wallowing was interrupted, though, by a husky voice from the cot below me.

"Frida?"

After only a small hesitation, I leaned over the edge of my

own cot and peered down at Aysche. "I didn't know you actually knew my name." Usually I was 'monster,' or 'Svand,' or 'D'ahvol savage'. I didn't know if I'd ever heard her use my name.

"I … I'm not … I don't know—"

"How to thank us?"

"No, I mean, no, I don't know what happened."

I had never heard her sound so uncertain. "The dragons kidnapped you and sold you into slavery on Lamruil. The savage Svand siblings arrived just in time to rescue you before you were sold at auction into some elven household."

"Sold? Slavery? My uncle—"

"As far as we can tell, Luthair had nothing to do with it."

"Where are you taking me?"

"You're along for the ride for now." The cot creaked as I shifted, preparing myself to show her a bit of kindness she had never shown me. "But we'll find a way to get you home. Or wherever you want to go. I promise."

She nodded without thanking me, and her eyes grew distant again.

I withdrew back over the edge, but there was one more thing I needed to know. "Do I need to worry about you stabbing me in the back while I sleep?"

"No." I could hear the smile in her voice, a rarity for her. "Not tonight, anyway."

"Truce?" I smiled at the ceiling.

"Truce," she answered.

I spent the rest of the night drifting in and out of a restless sleep. Once, I woke to check on Aysche only to find Erik already sitting with her, talking to her in low whispers. Arun's cot across from me was empty. I turned my back to the room and went back to sleep.

Captain Wynleth came for me in the morning, waking me before anyone else. To be frank, she was the last person I wanted to see first thing in the morning, but there she was, leaning over me, dark circles beneath her eyes.

"What?" I snapped. Our cabin had no windows and was dark, so I had no way of even knowing what time it was.

"There's a plateau ahead. I need to know if this is it."

I followed her to the deck. Arun was already—or still? — there, though Renwick was the one holding the wheel. He offered me a smile but I turned away, chasing the captain as she made her way to the front of the ship. A plateau loomed over the clouds. There was something familiar about it, and as we drew nearer, I made out the shape of a fence and a burned guardhouse beside the gate.

My chest was burning, and I thought it was from the shock of seeing this place again, but then I realized it was the rock in my vest pocket, where it sat beside the closed compass that hung around my neck. I pulled it out, barely able to touch it for fear of burning my hand. The whole thing was lit up.

I moaned. "It can't be."

Captain Wynleth looked down at the stone. "Seems like it is."

Arun appeared then, squinting at the plateau. "Is that…?"

I nodded. "Captain, can you take us below the veil?"

She scoffed. "Are you crazy? Do you know what's below the veil?"

"More than most. But I need to confirm where we are."

Even though she looked like she wanted to argue, she surprisingly bit her tongue and returned to the helm. After a few tense, silent moments, we began to descend.

When we were completely immersed in the white clouds of the veil and couldn't see anyone else, Arun turned to me. "Are you okay?"

"Fine," I said curtly. I told myself I was glad for the reminder of who I was. Glad that I would be able to push him away before he got any closer.

"You don't seem fine."

Then we were below the veil and there it was: the one place I'd been so desperate to leave for years. Barepost was a bowl of brown dust, hazy in the light of the rising sun. Without looking at him, I said, "Well, I guess I've been better."

Captain Wynleth took us back up and hovered at the edge of the higher plateau where Arun had left the *Iron Duchess* when he'd come to Barepost the first time.

Arun eyed the area dubiously as she sat her ship down in the clearing. "Last time I docked here, Luthair killed my crew and destroyed my ship." He didn't mention that his crew had been a group of delinquent dragons.

But the captain wasn't concerned. "He can try. My crew is a little more dangerous than they might look."

As if to prove her point, Renwick took a seat on the bowsprit beside Stiarna and began sharpening a knife he'd pulled from some hidden place against a small whetstone. The other men were disembarking, setting up tents, and gathering firewood.

"Maybe I should stay," Arun said to no one in particular.

I hated the tightening in my chest that his words caused. "You can do what you like."

Erik and Estrid appeared with Aysche trailing behind them. She was dressed in Estrid's spare set of clothes and looked incredibly uncomfortable in the too-big breeches. She kept tugging at the waistband and pulling the tunic down in an attempt to cover herself. Her hair, still unwashed, was pulled back in a tight, braided knot in the Ahvoli style.

I raised my eyebrows at her.

"Don't. Say. Anything." Her voice was regaining its former fire.

Laughing, I said, "Looks like we'll be taking you home sooner than we thought."

She held her arms out at her side and looked down at herself. "Fine with me. At least I'll be able to change into something more…"

"Suitable?" Estrid offered, shooting the girl a warning look before she could insult the only clothes available to her in front of their former owner.

Aysche, to my surprise, looked cowed. "Yes. Suitable."

Erik took Aysche by the elbow, and to my surprise, the girl didn't pull away from him. "I'll take Aysche home. It will give me the opportunity to speak to Luthair and make things right between us."

My eyes darted over to Estrid and she shrugged. I didn't think that was such a clever idea. Honestly, I would be fine dropping Aysche at the gate and never seeing her uncle again. But if Estrid was allowing it, then I wouldn't object. Luthair couldn't do anything to Erik, not anymore. He himself had made the bargain and lost the fight that freed Erik from his life-debt, even if it wasn't the way Erik would have preferred to do it.

I nodded at my brother and called to the griffin, who stood lazily, stretched, and then trotted over to where I stood. "She'll be our fastest way down."

Erik eyed the creature suspiciously but agreed.

Aysche was more reluctant. When Stiarna approached her, they eyed each other cautiously, like two animals sizing each other up before a fight. Thankfully, though, neither decided the other was worth it and Stiarna turned away with a small huff.

We walked the path back to the edge of the plateau. The bodies had been cleared, but the ground was still stained red-brown with blood in places. The guardhouse that had burned after a galestone pistol had exploded was a blackened skeleton. There were no signs of any life. Stiarna took Erik and Aysche down first. I heard a sharp intake of breath as she leapt from the cliffside, but both of them managed not to scream. She came back for Estrid and me and we soared down, my legs lodged behind her powerful wings and Estrid's arms around my waist.

The four of us moved toward the town in silence. I didn't

know about everyone else, but this place certainly brought back some unwelcome memories. Not only that, but as we drew nearer, I felt increasingly anxious for reasons I couldn't quite put my finger on. Outside the gates, I checked the rock. It still wanted us to go inside, so we approached the open gate with caution. But no one stopped us. The guards watched us pass but did not call to us or ask us our business here. It felt strangely like walking into a trap.

"Do you want to announce yourself to the guards?" Erik asked Aysche. The guards had not differentiated her from us.

Aysche put a hand on his arm. "No. I'll stick with you. I can't trust them anymore."

I didn't know if it was just the changing light of the morning sun, or if Erik's cheeks really did flush pink. It was strange to see them this way. He'd always thought her spoiled, and she'd always hated us unequivocally. But if anyone knew that there were some things in life that changed a person's outlook, it was us. And we wouldn't begrudge Aysche the right to do the same.

The streets were packed with morning crowds as everyone moved to work or went to the market to buy food for the day's meals. Some people noticed us with leery glances, while still others called good-naturedly to my brother, who still had Aysche hanging off his arm. Estrid and I walked behind them, rolling our eyes at each other. Every now and then, I ducked into an alley to orient the compass and check the rock, but every time, it kept us moving through town. It seemed silly to hide every time I wanted to look at it, but the last thing I needed was someone seeing and it getting back to Savarah that I had a special rock guiding me on my mission. Even if she didn't know what that mission was, I knew she would try to stop it.

We were weaving through a particularly crowded street when Estrid bumped into a man's shoulder. The man wheeled on her, fists clenched. Estrid held up her hands and took a step back.

"Watch where you're going, D'ahvol," the man spat at my sister.

I scowled at him over Estrid's shoulder. "It was an accident."

"Well, you should be more careful."

But I wasn't listening to the man anymore. I was listening to the crowd. The sound of bickering and general malcontent crashed over me like a wave. It seemed to originate from the very direction the stone wanted me to go. I stepped aside, pulling Estrid with me. Erik and Aysche followed. We ducked beneath the eaves of the nearby shop, even Stiarna, who wrapped her tail around herself to keep it out of the street.

"Do you feel it?" I asked.

Estrid nodded. "Yes. I don't like it. It feels like…"

"I know." It felt like Savarah. The stone was burning hot in my hand, the light still pointing in the same direction. "What do we do?"

Erik side-eyed Aysche, who was unusually quiet. "We need to find Luthair."

"No, *you* want to find Luthair. I want to follow this stone to the heir and then get out of here."

"Luthair knows everything there is to know about what happens in Barepost," Erik argued. "If Savarah is here, he'll know. And then we'll know how to avoid her."

The commotion around us grew louder. Someone stumbled out of the door beside us, nose bloody.

"I think it's too late for that." I dragged my siblings down the nearest alleyway, and we pressed ourselves against the wall, Erik tucking Aysche out of sight behind him. Then the three of us peered around the corner.

There she was, unmistakable in the same white dress she'd been wearing when I'd last seen her falling from the airship. But that was the only thing about her that was the same. She was openly manipulating people around her, laying her hands on arms and shoulders, creating skirmishes with a touch or a look. I guessed she was done with the good girl act.

Beside her was an elf in a fine pink gown, gold wire twisting around the points of her ears. It was Tsarra Trisfina, and she was laughing right along with her friend at the chaos around them.

"If this doesn't draw that rat-faced governor out of hiding," Savarah was saying as they passed our hiding place, "I don't know what will."

CHAPTER 5

We waited until they were out of sight to run to the opposite end of the alley, where we emerged on a familiar street that was empty and free of fighting humans. We turned left and ducked inside the first door, leaving Stiarna to watch the entrance.

The inside of the Gold Mine Inn and Pub was mostly empty this time of day. Gerves, the innkeeper, was sweeping the hearth and looked up when we blew inside. There was only one patron at the bar, and he got up and left at the sight of us, slamming the door behind him.

Gerves's eyes went and he searched our faces. I knew he was looking for his daughter, Grissall, who had left Barepost with us after the ur'gel attack.

"She's not here," I told him quickly, trying to head off any panic attacks, "but she's safe." I'd left her with Lunla at the temple at the priest's instructions, but I would have to fill him in later.

He slumped in obvious relief. "What are you doing here?" Crossing to the door, he peeked out and then shut it again, dropping the latch into place. "If Luthair sees you, he'll imprison you all. Maybe even execute you, depending on his mood."

I grabbed Aysche's arm and tugged her forward. She stumbled a bit but righted herself, glaring at me. "He won't. We have insurance."

Erik started to protest but I cut him off with a look.

Gerves stared at Aysche for a long moment. "Is that ... is that his niece?"

Aysche squared her shoulders and raised her chin. "Yes."

"Hm," Gerves grunted. "We thought you'd died in the valley after the ur'gel attack. Your uncle sent search parties, but no one had seen you since you left the gates."

She slumped a little, dropping her superior demeanor that somehow didn't seem to fit her anymore. "I went beyond the gates? Willingly?"

"I believe so, yes."

I turned to her. "We saw you after the battle. You were not captured, if that's what you were thinking. In fact, you were hurling curses at me, very much yourself."

But there was something else, someone who had been there with us, in fact. Savarah. Could she have been influencing Aysche? Sent her out into the valley just for her own amusement, even when she wasn't there to watch it? Just because she could? Knowing what I did about her now, I had no doubt that she would. Just like the heir, anyone's power could be used for either good or evil, depending on what the wielder decided. And Savarah was decidedly evil.

And I couldn't leave even Luthair to her mercy. Besides, Erik was probably right about Luthair knowing more about Barepost than anyone. If there was something here to do with the heir, he would likely know about it. Now we just had to find him, which wasn't too easy if Savarah's earlier comment had been any indication.

"We have to find him," Erik said, putting voice to my own

reluctant thoughts. "His life is in danger. The whole town is in danger. Do you know where he is?"

Gerves shook his head. "He's laid low since the ur'gel attack."

Erik looked at me and then at Aysche. "Any idea where he might go?"

I shook my head, but Aysche looked thoughtful. "There is somewhere. But I'm not supposed to tell anyone."

Estrid rolled her eyes. She looked ready to back Aysche against the wall. "What are you not supposed to tell us?"

"If he's where I think he is, we need to get to the house on the ridge."

I shrugged, not wanting to fight with her, not anymore. It didn't hold the same joy for me as when she was at her best. "At least it's a start."

"Let's go then." Erik began to corral us out the door.

I slipped away from him and let the rest of the group leave before turning back to Gerves. "When Harbin comes back next, will you tell him … will you tell him that we made it out? Will you tell him about what happened?"

Gerves nodded. "Of course. When you next see Grissall, will you give her my love?"

"She doesn't need me to." I smiled, and then lifted a hand in farewell.

But before I could follow the rest of them out the door, they were barreling back inside. I stumbled back against the bar. Gerves was already pulling out a metal rod from below the counter, having given his galestone pistol to us before we left.

I righted myself. "What is it?"

Erik spun me by the shoulders and pushed me to the back. We all piled behind the counter. "We can't go out the front door. The fighting…"

He didn't need to finish. A body crashed through the door and landed sprawled on the floor. It was a young man. Another young man came through after him and leapt on him, pummeling his already bloody face.

Stiarna was right behind them, hissing as she slinked over the counter and crouched there, her hackles raised. I put an apologetic hand on her neck.

The noise drifting in through the now-open door told me there was more of the same on the street. If it was this bad, that meant Savarah had to be close.

I turned to Gerves. "Is there a back door?"

"This way." He motioned for us to follow him through the kitchen. There was a woman I'd never seen before standing at a wash basin, her sleeves rolled up. "Barricade the door," Gerves told her. "Whatever you do, don't go out there."

She nodded, wiping her hands on her apron.

Gerves opened a rickety wooden door that led to a back alley. The small street was filthy, dishwater and who knew what else running down the ditch in the middle. We didn't care. The important thing was that it was empty.

We spilled out into the alley, thanking Gerves for his help.

Erik clapped a hand on the innkeeper's shoulder. "Will you be okay? Should we stay and help defend the Gold Mine?"

"No. It will be even worse for us all if you're discovered here. Go. Be smart. Be safe."

The door shut and the four of us were on our own.

Aysche whirled on me with a glare and her arms lashed out, pushing me back. Only because she caught me off guard, I slammed against the stone wall of the inn, my teeth clattering together. I heard Stiarna growl from somewhere close by.

"Don't think you can use me as some kind of bargaining tool with my uncle," she growled.

A familiar anger rose inside of me. Before she knew what had happened, I grabbed her and turned, knocking her against the wall and keeping her there with an arm across her throat. My other hand searched for the small knife I knew she carried.

She croaked and gagged, fingers scraping against my arm.

"Don't think you can put your hands on me and get away with it. Ever." I bared my teeth at her.

It was Erik who pulled me off, tossing me to the side. My boot landed in a brown puddle of something gross that I didn't really want to think about.

"Glad to see you're feeling more like yourself, though," I said to Aysche as I scraped my boot against a fairly clean cobblestone.

Erik huffed. "It's not her. It's Savarah."

I thought in this case, it was probably a little bit of both. But I didn't get a chance to say so because Erik was herding us down the alley and then we turned into another. It spit us out on the main road a few blocks ahead of the fighting, so we made a break for it, running down the path that would eventually lead to the house on the ridge.

Luthair's enormous house sat on a ridge above Barepost, on the edge of the mountain that also housed his mine, the mine that supported the entire town. It had glass windows and gas lamps, luxuries that almost no one else could afford. But he saw himself as the savior of Barepost and deserving of the finer things.

We followed the path to the front door. After several knocks, Missus, Luthair's housemaid, opened the door, blinking out at us.

"Aysche? Is that you?"

Aysche lifted her chin a bit in what I was beginning to recognize as a defensive gesture. "Yes. I need to speak to my uncle."

"He's not here. I already told the golden-haired lass."

"I expect I know where he is." Aysche narrowed her eyes at the older woman.

"He is not to be disturbed," Missus hissed, lowering her voice.

Erik shouldered his way to the front, never one to leave the talking to anyone else. "He'll want to be disturbed for this."

Without waiting for permission, we filed inside the grand foyer, even the griffin. Estrid, the only one of us who had never been inside, gaped at the winding staircase and the tall ceilings. I tugged her forward, following Aysche down the hall on the left. I'd been down this hall before, and knew it led to the kitchens and then down a narrow staircase to a bathing room.

If Luthair was in the bathing room, I could wait. There weren't enough emergencies in the world—

But Aysche barreled right in. I peeked around the threshold and was glad to find the room empty, though still as magnificent as it had been last time I'd seen it. The bath in the middle of the room sat empty, but the room was still warm, likely due to its proximity to the hot springs. Thinking about the hot springs, and being there with Arun, made me grin stupidly. I tried to get myself under control. I had no business thinking about him, not when he was so clearly interested in Captain Wynleth.

We followed Aysche to the back of the room, where she pushed on the corner of the wooden plank wall and it slid open, revealing the mouth of a stone tunnel. After taking an already lit lamp off the wall, Aysche ducked inside without hesitation, followed by Estrid, but Erik and I—both having been in the mines before—hesitated. We knew what could wait for us in these tunnels, what kinds of monsters and dangers waited for us.

"After you." Erik waved a hand at me.

Sighing, I stepped through. I was glad to find that the ceiling was at least tall enough to accommodate me, even if Erik had to duck slightly as he entered behind me. The tunnel had several off-shooting corridors, but Aysche kept us going straight until we came to a heavy stone door. She heaved it open and light poured out of the room beyond.

We gathered in the doorway and took in the sight before us.

It was an office, with stone walls and a red rug on the polished stone floor. There was a desk and a bookshelf laden with leather-bound books, and a cot against one wall. Two chairs were set before a hearth, where a fire burned.

From behind the heavy desk, Luthair stood, his mouth dropping open at the sight of us. It felt nice to finally leave him speechless.

I took a step inside the room. "Your life is in danger," I said, my voice bouncing off of the walls. "You need to leave. Now."

CHAPTER 6

"Well, I wasn't in danger until the lot of you barged in." He bustled past us and closed the door. "How do you know you weren't followed?"

Aysche rolled her eyes at her uncle. "Because we used the passageway through the house."

As if seeing his niece for the first time, Luthair grabbed her shoulders and pulled her into a hug. "And how are you alive? What happened to you?"

She freed herself from his arms. "Apparently I wandered into the valley to get eaten by monsters at the whim of some mind-controlling freak."

"Not mind—" Erik started to interrupt but snapped his mouth shut at a glare from Aysche.

"Instead, I was captured by your dragon friends and sold into slavery."

Luthair turned his gaze on me. "I assume you played some part in this."

I smirked at him. "The part where I rescued her when you couldn't."

"We," Erik interrupted again. "*We* rescued her."

Luthair looked unimpressed. To his niece, he said, "Well done, bringing them back here, at least. Now I can lock them up like I should have done three years ago."

That was all I needed to hear. I hooked my arm around Aysche's shoulders and with my other hand, held her own knife to her throat. I'd taken it from where it had been strapped to her belt when we'd been scuffling in the alley, just in case. It had been so she couldn't pull it on me, but it would serve another purpose now.

To my surprise, though, Luthair didn't step back and hold his hands up in surrender, scared for his niece's life. No. He laughed. I should have known to expect such a nonsensical reaction from a man like him, but it still caught me off guard.

"Onen help me, but I've missed you."

I ground my teeth together and tightened my grip on Aysche. She grunted in protest.

Luthair remained unaffected. He walked back to his desk and began shuffling through papers. "My earlier offer still stands. Barepost could use a woman like you. *I* could use a woman like you."

I shoved Aysche away from me. Erik caught her, dusting her off and looking her over for puncture wounds. I hadn't given her any. I took two long strides across the room and slammed my hands down on his desk.

"If you stay hidden down here like a coward, it's only a matter of time before Barepost is destroyed. Then, you'll be discovered and killed or captured. Is that what you want to happen, after all your hard work?" Talking to him was a lot like talking to the elven king, but I knew Luthair. When Luthair had conquered Barepost, it had been a lawless free-for-all. He took pride in the city, even if he had to rule it with an iron fist. "And the longer I'm here," I added, "the worse it will be."

That got his attention at least. "What are you talking about?"

"I can show you better than I can tell you. But we need to go up."

He scrutinized me for a long moment before nodding. "Follow me."

Aysche and Erik stayed behind, Aysche to get cleaned up and changed, and Erik to stand guard over her. The Aysche of a few weeks ago never would have allowed him to even be close to her, but this Aysche blushed and allowed him to follow her back through the tunnel toward the house. I wasn't sure I liked where that was going but I didn't get a chance to object.

Luthair led us in the opposite direction, deeper into the tunnels beneath the mine. He fell into step beside me, Estrid and Stiarna several paces behind us.

"I could …" He cleared his throat. "I could protect you, you know? If you are in some kind of trouble."

I very nearly laughed before realizing that he was trying to show me kindness. It was my turn to study him. He wasn't terrible to look at, even if he was at least a decade my senior. He was tall and lean, with sharp features and a serious face. One that had spent so much time sneering at me for the last three years that I wasn't sure what to make of the vulnerability I saw on it as we walked through the tunnel. Now that I wasn't under his thumb and he couldn't control me through my brother, it was like he was trying another tactic, one that had never occurred to him before. A small part of me wished he'd been this way from the start, that he'd saved my brother out of goodness instead of an ulterior motive. That he'd kept us in Barepost because it was what was best for us, not what was best for him.

But a few kind words and my own broken heart couldn't erase the cruelties he'd shown us the last few years.

"I don't need protection," I told him finally.

We came upon a metal gate set in the stone wall. It slid aside at Luthair's touch and revealed a small wooden room no bigger than a few square feet. We peered inside.

"What is this?" I asked.

"A pulley-elevator," he answered. "Like at the wharf."

"But we're inside the mountain."

He beamed at us. "Yes, we are. We've carved a shaft through the mountain that reaches the very top of the plateau. Where we did battle last."

I smirked. "You mean where I kicked your—"

"Shall we?" Luthair held an arm out and we stepped onto the platform. He slid the door shut and took hold of the rope dangling from the overhead pulley. We took turns hauling ourselves up, and while it was arduous work, it was certainly easier than scaling the side of the mountain and fighting off cliff monsters while doing it.

The top of the pulley elevator was just beyond the guard-house we'd burned, in a small building that looked more like an outhouse. The four of us stumbled out, Stiarna bounding away into the trees. Estrid perched on a nearby log to wait for us.

Smoothing down his robes, Luthair looked over at me. "Now, show me what's going on."

We trampled through the trees and emerged on the eastern-most edge of the plateau that looked down over Barepost. The clouds were thin. The city was visible. So was the unrest. Even if I couldn't make out Savarah from up here, her influence was obvious. Crowds of people yelling and shoving. Broken stalls in the market and grown men rolling in the dusty streets, hands wrapped around each other's throats. Shouts of anger reached us even up here.

I watched Luthair for a reaction.

He leaned back from the edge. "Yes, the lawlessness has gotten worse since the ur'gel attack. I'll get it back under control. Is that all?"

I shook my head. "It's not just that. It's Savarah, Dag'draath's general. She's the one causing this unrest, and she's looking for you."

"Savarah? The great temptress? Impossible. She's imprisoned."

I raised my eyebrows at him. "With the ur'gels?"

He grunted, his eyes still on Barepost below us. "If what you're saying is true, then this is worse than I thought."

"No kidding. This isn't something you can quell with force. Even your men are involved." I pointed to the gate where two guards in black were squaring off against one another, weapons drawn.

He held up a finger, unmoved by the scene. "But it's still not hopeless. I know why she's looking for me. She's foolish to have come here. Pride goeth before a fall, and all that."

Now it was my turn to be confused. "What are you talking about?"

"During the Dark War, the humans created a device to keep her at bay. I just happen to have it in my possession."

"What?" I whipped my head toward him. "How do you just happen to have this item? And how does she know?"

"It was in the possession of the Oubliee for centuries," Luthair explained. "They traded it to a D'ahvol man in exchange for his services, and this man gave it to my sister as a gift before her death. It was the only thing he owned. All that he had to give to her, and she, in turn, gave him a son. It cost her her life. Not a fair trade, in my opinion." He looked up at me, his face emotionless. "Although it appears it may now come in handy."

I was speechless even as my mind raced. Haklang, the foreman in the mines, had to be the D'ahvol he was talking about. Luthair had sentenced Haklang to life in the mines after his affair with Luthair's older sister was discovered, and sent his infant son, Xalph, down with him. Until we'd freed Xalph a few weeks ago, the boy had never even seen the sun.

"And how does she know you have it?" I asked.

"I might have mentioned it at a co-op meeting once or twice."

Bragged about it, more like. He was a collector of the rare and beautiful, after all. Why have something if he couldn't show it off? "Pride goes before a fall," I muttered.

He smiled unashamedly.

It occurred to me that perhaps this was why the stone brought us back here. Maybe the first step to finding the heir was to disable Savarah.

"Name your price," I said abruptly.

Luthair's eyes knitted together in confusion.

"What will it take for you to hand over the device? What would it cost me?"

"You already know what I want from you."

Yes, I did. He wanted to add me to his collection of finery. He wanted to keep me in his house on the ridge and dress me in silk clothes that he could take off me at will.

"And you already know my answer."

He held up one finger. "One night, then. Just you and me."

There was no humor in his voice. He was being completely serious. Savarah was bad, but was she that bad? I didn't think so. "Not going to happen. Besides, Savarah wants me maybe more than she wants you. If she finds us both together … we might as well just hand the world over to Dag'draath."

"Why is she after you?"

I pressed my lips together, deciding whether or not to answer him.

He saw my indecision and, to my surprise, changed the subject. "Erik still feels indebted to me, doesn't he?"

It was my turn to look confused.

"I'll tell him, I will confirm to him that he is free of his life-debt, if you'll tell me the truth about what's really going on. What it is that has my people in danger?"

Though I had no real reason to trust him, I did. He was mean-spirited at times, and unwaveringly strict, but in the end, he wanted only to do what was right for his people. It pained me to think it, but he was honorable when it came down to it. That was why Erik had honored his debt to him, and why Erik needed to make sure he was truly clear of it before being able to move on. The two of them were so very different from each other but were still the two most respectable men I knew.

"Savarah thinks I'm the heir of Onen Suun. That I have the power to free him from the prison or repair it and keep him and his minions there."

"She thinks you are, but you're not?"

I shook my head. "I'm a decoy. But I'm also the only one who can find the true heir. So, either way, if Savarah captures me..." I didn't need to finish. We both knew what would happen then.

He turned his back on Barepost and began back down the path to the elevator shaft. "I'll give you the device," he called over his shoulder.

"But I'm not—"

"For free." He held a branch back for me to pass. "Now, let's go get it before she does."

CHAPTER 7

We left Estrid and Stiarna on the plateau with instructions to return to the *Wind Wraith* and prepare it for departure. Then Luthair and I rode down the elevator shaft in silence, taking turns holding the rope. It was much quicker than the ascent, the rope burning my palms as I let it out slowly. I could feel Luthair's eyes on me, but I ignored him, not wanting to know what he thought about my predicament or my connection to the heir. I just wanted to get the device, get Erik, and get out of there. Hopefully for good this time.

I followed Luthair through the winding tunnels back past his office and into the bathing room. We took the stairs up into the narrow corridor, hurried past the kitchen, and through the grand lobby, where Missus was wringing her hands.

"Governor, sir," she called as we pass. "They're coming."

We hadn't noticed it before in our haste, but now that we stood still and listened, we could hear what sounded like chanting. Like a mob making its way up the path to the house on the ridge. I'd wanted to light the place on fire my fair share of times, but I never thought I'd live to see the day when his own people turned on him. Of course, it was because of Savarah, but that didn't make it any less surprising.

I recognized the hall of bedrooms where I'd spent the night once before at the top of the winding staircase. Erik stood outside one of the doors. When he saw us, he cracked the door open without looking inside, and said to its occupant, "Aysche? They're back."

Luthair's niece emerged a moment later wearing a dark blue gown, her eyes lined with kohl and her cheeks pink with rouge. But her hair was still done in the tight Ahvoli braids.

Erik touched one of them. "You kept them. I'm glad."

I thought I might have blushed about as red and Aysche did.

The door at the end of the hall opened to reveal a bedroom as large as our entire house back in Bor'sur. At the foot of the four-poster bed was a familiar trunk. I crossed to it without being invited and unlatched the lid.

"Your things." Luthair appeared beside me, looking down into the trunk's sparse contents with me. "I kept them, in case you ever came back for them."

"I'm surprised Gerves let you take them."

He shrugged. "Doesn't have much of a choice, does he? I am the governor, after all."

On the night stand beside his bed was a wooden box locked with a metal dial. Leaning low over the box, Luthair spun the dial and popped off the box's lid. After rifling around for a moment, he pulled out a necklace and handed it to me.

"That's it?" I studied the silver heart on its chain.

"That's it." He snapped the box shut so I couldn't see what other treasures he had squirreled away that might someday come in handy when saving the world.

Erik looked between me and Luthair, then asked, "Is my life-debt truly cleared? Not because of the bargain my sister struck with you, but because of the work that I did for you?"

Luthair sighed but nodded, keeping to our agreement. "Many times over, yes. You are free to go."

I tried not to see the hurt look that passed briefly over Aysche's face. I still wasn't used to her having feelings, after all. Especially not for my brother. Maybe her definition of monster had changed, though, these last few days.

There was a crash from outside. Luthair glanced out the large glass window across the room. "They're here. Quick, to the lobby. We'll be able to hold them off better from there."

We wasted no time returning to the lobby, passing Missus, who was stashing silver candlesticks and other valuables as if that were what mattered. I draped the necklace around my neck.

"What do I do?" I asked Luthair. "How do I use it?"

Luthair was in the middle of the room. His response was nearly drowned out by the sound of the mob outside banging on the door. "Take it and go. I'll hold them off. Aysche, get down to the safe room. Wait for me there."

Erik was already dragging Aysche away when she turned back to her uncle. "What if you don't come for me?"

Luthair opened his mouth and snapped it shut. He obviously didn't have an answer and wasn't one to make false promises.

It was my brother who finally spoke. "I'll stay with you."

"Erik," I objected.

He didn't look at me. "I'll stay with you until he comes. I'll make sure you're safe."

With a nod, she let him lead her down the hall that would take them to the bathing room and then into the mountain. I was meant to follow, but I paused in the dark of the corridor and looked back at Luthair. He stood in the middle of his foyer, his sword drawn and his face stoic. He nodded at Missus who swung the door open. I'd expected him to be swarmed by angry villagers, but instead, there was the sound of two pairs of footsteps echoing on the stone floor, and beyond that, an eerie silence.

I felt her before I saw her—the tightness in my chest, the ringing in my ears. All the bad memories came back to me. My siblings treating me like I wasn't one of them. Luthair holding us captive in Barepost. The deaths of the miners on the plateau. Arun smiling at Captain Wynleth. His empty cot. I covered my mouth with my hand to suppress the urge to scream.

Savarah approached Luthair casually, no weapon in her hands. But she didn't need a weapon. Her mind *was* her weapon. Tsarra Trisfina was on her other side, carrying two small knives in her hands. I wondered if she was here of her own free will, or if she was under Savarah's control.

"Governor," Savarah said by way of greeting.

Luthair didn't step back, to his credit. "Savarah."

The empath smiled slyly. "So, you know who I am."

"Of course." His eyes flickered to the door over her shoulder at something I couldn't see. "Your reputation precedes you."

"Then you know what I want." She was close to him, running a finger down his cheek.

"I have a pretty good idea."

"You have it, then?"

He looked down at his hands, as if surprised not to find the necklace dangling there. That was when I knew he was under her spell. "No. Not anymore."

Her nails dug into his shoulder, but he didn't flinch or pull away. The sword hung limp in his hand, useless against her.

I pulled the necklace out of my shirt and fumbled with it. How did it work? Did I have to be beside her? Touching her? In my vest pocket, the wayfinder's stone was ice-cold against my chest. I was so tired of magical objects that didn't come with any obvious instructions. How was I—someone who had no magic —supposed to figure this out?

"Where is it?" Savarah hissed, her anger barely concealed.

The mob she'd left at the door felt it too, and began to grow restless. I could hear grumbling and shuffling feet. Someone must have knocked into someone else because there was sudden shouting that ended with the sound of a fist against flesh.

Luthair lifted his head and began to turn toward my hiding place in the corridor. He was going to give me up, and the power to stop her was literally in my hands if I could just figure out—

A hinge. My fingers brushed against what felt like a small hinge in the silver heart. I dug my nail into the crease.

Savarah began to turn, following his line of sight.

The necklace—a locket, I realized—popped open, and a wave of blue light exploded out of it, sweeping over the room and out of the house.

My mouth dropped open and I looked up, but Savarah wasn't looking at me. I poked my head around the corner and saw what had her attention. The mob in the doorway was dispersing, people wandering away, scratching their heads in confusion, clapping hands on friend's backs, apologizing to each other.

Her army was deserting. Only Tsarra was left. Savarah seemed to realize this, because she grabbed Tsarra in a panic and held one of her own knives to the elf's throat.

"Savarah!" Tsarra gasped, fingers grappling at the pale white arm across her shoulders.

Savarah didn't even look at her. "Give it to me! Give it to me or the elf dies!"

Luthair was still for a long moment in that way I knew meant he was weighing his options. I'd seen that look on his face before. Of course, Savarah hadn't, so she didn't know to be afraid.

Then, quick as a snake lashing out at an unsuspecting rat, Luthair drove his sword into Tsarra's chest.

Savarah gasped and stepped backward. She was not hurt, but

surprised. I couldn't blame her. I'd known he was planning something but hadn't seen that coming in the least.

Tsarra stumbled toward him, still speared on the end of his sword, her eyes wide with shock. Blood bloomed on her dress.

Luthair braced his arm against her shoulder and tugged his sword free.

She collapsed to her knees, and then fell face-first against the floor.

Luthair turned his eyes on Savarah. "Get out," he said coolly. "Do not let me see you in my town again."

I didn't wait to see if she left. Instead, I turned and fled down the corridor. It was time to go. I was done with Barepost, for the last time.

CHAPTER 8

When I burst into the underground office, I came face-to-face with Erik's sword. I knocked it aside with my gloved hand.

"What happened?" he asked, sheathing the weapon.

Aysche emerged from where she'd been behind the desk. "Is my uncle okay?"

"Your uncle?" I laughed at the idea that anything could possibly happen to Luthair. "He's fine." To Erik, I added, "He killed Tsarra."

His pale eyebrows knit together over his eyes. "Tsarra? Why Tsarra?"

"To spare her."

Whirling around, I found Luthair in the doorway. His sword was still in his hand but had been wiped clean. I didn't want to know with what.

"To spare her *what*?" I asked.

"She was Savarah's next victim. She likes to play with her food. The elf was nothing but a tool, something to hold over those of you with hearts."

I noticed that he hadn't said those of *us*. Ignoring him, I beckoned to Erik. "Let's go."

He didn't move. "Frida, I..."

"You what?"

He squared his shoulders. "I'm not going."

"Not going where?" I didn't understand. I looked at him, then down at Aysche who was peeking out from behind him, then at Luthair, who shrugged.

"I'm staying in Barepost."

I narrowed my eyes and took a step toward him. "For a *girl*?"

"Because it's where I want to be."

"You want to be here? In Barepost?"

"It's not all bad," Luthair chimed in.

I glared at him. "It's awful."

"And maybe it is a little bit for a girl," Aysche added.

Erik grinned back at her. He was practically glowing. It was disgusting.

I decided to try a different tactic. "Estrid will be furious. She won't leave you."

"Estrid doesn't need me any more than you do. I trust you can convince her to go."

"Erik."

He crossed the room to where I stood in the doorway and put his hands on my shoulders. "There was never any guarantee that our destinies would take us in the same direction always. I was so lucky to have been given the opportunity to be your big brother, but here is where our paths diverge. The longer you stand here and argue with me, the more at risk your mission becomes."

My mission. Not his, not anymore. Part of me wanted to rage against Aysche, to blame her or Luthair. But I bit my anger back in an effort to see his reasoning. So instead, I asked, "What will you do?"

Erik looked to Luthair, who was also standing close by.

Close enough that he was able to reach up and finger the locket hanging around my neck.

"We're going to make more of these," he said.

"What? How?"

"It hasn't just been sitting in my room. I've been studying its composition, and at its core is ublarite, a mineral that is found in the depths of the mine." He turned the locket over in his fingers, his knuckles coming *awfully close* to my chest.

I pulled away and it slid out of his grasp.

He was unfazed, taking a step away. "It's difficult and dangerous to mine, but with your brother's consent, I would like him and Haklang to gather an extraction team. I will work with the local smiths on the settings."

"You should make as many as you can." I held up a finger to catch his attention. "This isn't a for-profit venture. Get them out into the world as quickly and as cheaply as possible."

Luthair looked sheepish, but Erik nodded. "She's right. As soon as Savarah discovers the source of the device, she and the ur'gels will return to shut down production in the most violent way possible."

"We will be ready for them," Luthair promised, an arm around his niece's shoulders. For once, the girl didn't look scared or like she was putting on a show. She looked prepared, ready to face whatever was coming as long as she had Luthair and Erik with her.

I would never admit I was a bit jealous of her.

"You'd better go," Erik said to me, nudging me toward the door. "Foregin willing, we will meet again."

I had never been a fan of the god of fate, but I wouldn't argue the point with Erik, not now. I clasped his hands in mine. "Be safe."

He raised his eyebrows at me. "Be brave."

When I walked away, I didn't look back.

The pulley-elevator was much harder to work by myself. I

had to take a break several minutes in, tying the rope off in a knot to keep me from falling back to the ground. By the time I reached the top, my arms, shoulders, and back burned with the effort. But it was a good distraction. It kept me from thinking about having to leave Erik behind, and having to tell Estrid that we were doing it.

Once in the clearing beside the burned guardhouse, I pulled the wayfinder's stone from my pocket and flipped open the compass beside it, spinning until I was facing the north. The western point of the stone lit up, burning hot against my thumb. Barepost—and Erik—were to the east. The ship was waiting for me through the trees to the west.

I snapped it closed and stuffed everything away, the locket and the compass knocking into each other beneath my vest, the stone warm in my pocket. Then I trampled through the trees back to where the ship was. It was strange to be alone, and even stranger to think when I returned home, it would be without Erik. For the first time, I wondered at my father's reaction when only two of us returned home. Would it be disappointment instead of joy?

The farther I walked, the more I thought about it, trying to picture the moment my father gathered me up in his arms again. I didn't think he would be upset. He'd always encouraged us to forge our own paths, and perhaps even accepted that we wouldn't be together forever.

"Look up, my star," he'd said to me. "We will always be under the same sky."

Maybe he had never expected any of us to return.

The deck of the *Wind Wraith* was busy with sailors dashing to their posts. The sound of an unfurling sail met me as Estrid took my hand and helped me over the railing.

She looked past me. "Where is Erik?"

"He's not coming." I kept walking even though I knew she'd want more information.

Her hand on my shoulder snapped me backward. "He's not coming? Where is he?"

"He's staying in Barepost."

She drew her sword and turned back to the edge. "That blasted Luthair, I'll kill him if—"

It was my turn to stop her. I grabbed her wrist. "Put the sword away. It was his decision."

Renwick approached then, looking warily between us. "The captain wants to know if we're ready to go."

"Yes," I confirmed, releasing Estrid's arm. "Tell her to head west."

"We're not leaving without Erik," Estrid argued as Renwick hurried away.

"We have no choice. He isn't coming."

The sound of the gangplank scraping on the wooden deck punctuated my point. Estrid ran to stop the sailors but she was too late. The ship was rising, and the sun was sinking. Captain Wynleth would want to get off the ground before night fell and the cliff monsters emerged. To escape Estrid's wrath, I skirted away from her, moving to the front of the ship, not letting myself look around for Arun. I took a seat beside Stiarna near the bow and leaned against her muscular body. She nipped at my hair with her beak and I tilted my head back, a breeze touching my cheeks.

Look up, my star.

So I did, and for the first time in my life, saw nothing but darkness.

CHAPTER 9

I stayed there all night, curling into Stiarna's warmth when the wind made me shiver. I could hear Estrid arguing with Captain Wynleth about turning around and going back for Erik. I didn't intervene, and the captain held her ground, keeping the ship up in the air and headed west, racing Aupra, the smaller of Iynia's two moons.

When she finally disappeared and the sun peeked over the horizon behind us, hands pulled me from my hiding place and tossed me onto the deck. My ax was in my hands before I'd even regained my feet. I turned on Estrid, who had no weapons drawn but her hands were balled into fists at her side, her chest heaving. There were dark circles under her eyes.

"How could you?" she growled at me.

I put the ax back into my belt. "I didn't have a choice."

"You should have stayed. How could you let him stay behind on his own?"

The thought hadn't really occurred to me. "I couldn't stay in Barepost. My destiny lies elsewhere."

Estrid rolled her eyes. "Your *destiny*, how could I forget?"

I pressed my lips together, trying to fight back the tightness gripping my chest. I couldn't even blame this one on Savarah. This anger, this cruelty—it was all Estrid. "You have no idea how hard it was for me to let him go, but it was what he wanted."

"Before all of this—before your destiny—you never would have left him behind." She paced back and forth a few steps at a time, keeping me cornered against the railing. "You've changed, and not for the better."

I held my arms out to the side. "Of course, I've changed. We all have. The entire world is changing. Ur'gels and Dag'-draath and dreamwalkers! This must be done. I have to find the heir. I have to save...," I trailed off. It sounded ludicrous even to my own ears, but Estrid caught it like a dog with a bone.

"Save the world," she sneered. "Even if it costs you your family."

Before I could respond, Estrid lunged at me. She wrapped her hands in my vest and pressed me against the railing. All it would take was for the wood to snap and we would both plummet to our deaths.

As quickly as she'd grabbed me, though, she let go. I righted myself, smoothing down my shirt, and found myself staring at Captain Wynleth's dark, stormy eyes. She stood between us, a hand to Estrid's chest, the other on her sheathed sword.

"This ends now," she said in a low, menacing voice. "Unless you want to die at the end of my sword, you can continue this fight off of my ship."

From the way she was scowling at me, I almost expected Estrid to call the captain's bluff. But after a tense moment, she took a few steps back, her arms out at her sides as if to say, "See? No problems here." Even if her face said otherwise.

I didn't want to test her, so I slipped away from the two of them and descended into the bowels of the ship. I didn't typically like spending time below deck, but it was better than facing Estrid and her mood, so I ducked down the stairs and slid aside the door to our sleeping quarters.

Where I was met with a bare, muscled back that ended in narrow hips and low-slung linen pants. Arun turned, and suddenly I was staring at a bare, muscled chest instead.

"Hi," he said, offering me a small smile.

I tried to speak but found my throat very dry, so I coughed instead, managing to cover my mouth with my hand but still not looking away.

He had his shirt in his hands, and he slid it over his head, leaving the neck unlaced as he tied his hair back with a leather thong.

"Good morning," I finally managed, only after he was mostly dressed. It pained me I couldn't control my body's reaction to him, even when my head told me it was a stupid and pointless attraction.

He sat on a cot and began lacing up his boots. "What are you up to?"

"Hiding from Estrid." I sat across from him.

"Because of Erik?" he asked. So, he had been on the deck and witnessed that whole scene.

I nodded in confirmation. "What about you? Why are you down here?"

"Hiding from Quynn." He finished lacing his boots and sat back, the cot creaking beneath him.

"Why?" I asked, hating that he'd mentioned her name.

Apparently oblivious to my discomfort, he shook his head. "I don't know what I'm supposed to do if I can't give the orders. She's already threatened to lop off my hands if I touch her ship one more time."

I grunted and looked away from him, wrapping my arms around myself, a fruitless effort to try to keep my spitefulness contained.

He leaned forward, his elbows on his knees. "What?"

"Nothing."

Laughing, he pushed himself off his cot and spun around, falling beside me onto mine. The cot rocked and I tipped over against him. He wrapped an arm around my shoulders and shook me. I took a deep breath. He smelled so good, damp and freshly bathed but still salty, like the sea air.

"What is it? What has you all distant and quiet with me? I thought… Well, I thought we were … you know."

"Friends?" I offered.

He tilted his head back and forth, then slowly said, "Yeah, friends."

I was so stupid. "I just, I wanted to give you and the captain your space. To become … friends." *Or something more*, I added in my head but didn't dare say aloud.

He laughed again, the sound making me want to reach over and punch him in the face. How was it that I could face down a massive blazetaur without hesitation, but talking to Arun about my feelings had me terrified? It seemed a little backward. I surprised myself by wishing for the first time that I had a girl-friend, someone like Aysche, who I could talk to about things like this. I didn't think Estrid would want to hear it, especially not right now.

Finally, Arun said, "Quynn is like a cave dragon."

I remembered encountering a cave dragon with him when he and I had been exploring the mine for an escape route. "What do you mean?"

"You don't befriend a cave dragon. You hold still and let it sniff you, and hope it doesn't bite your head off."

That comparison seemed surprisingly accurate. I just hadn't known he felt that way, too. "So, you and Quynn aren't…?"

"Friends? No, I wouldn't say we were friends."

The feeling of his arm around my shoulders changed, no longer playful as his thumb stroked my arm and my heart picked up speed, jumping into my throat. He was so close. All I had to do was turn my head and tilt my chin up. I clasped my hands in my lap and stared at them, afraid to move, afraid to touch him, but wanting desperately for him to keep touching me.

The sound of boots on the ladder was all it took for us to shoot apart from each other, both of us leaping to our feet and moving to opposite sides of the room. That was how Renwick found us, studiously not looking at each other.

He looked between us, shook his head, and then fixed his gaze on me. "The captain wants to know if there's a new heading."

Nodding, I drew the stone and compass from my shirt and oriented them. The direction had shifted slightly. "Northwest," I told him.

He nodded and turned to go, but as he did, the light faded.

"Wait," I said.

He paused and looked back at me.

Arun crossed the room, looking over my shoulder at the stone. "What is it?"

Not only was the stone not glowing, but all the warmth had faded out of it, as if I'd dropped it into an ice chest. I remembered what had happened the last time the stone had gone cold to the touch.

Looking up at Arun and Renwick, I said, "The ship is in danger."

CHAPTER 10

The three of us stormed up the ladder and crossed the deck to the helm in a flurry of shouting. The captain looked down at us, stunned, but only briefly.

"Quiet, all of you," she ordered. Then, pointing at me, "You. Go."

"The ship is in danger." I held the stone up as if she would be able to see the threat in its smooth surface. "The wayfinder's stone has gone cold. The last time that happened, we were attacked by ur'gels."

The mere mention of the monsters sent the sailors into a frenzy, shouting back and forth to each other and searching the skies.

But Quynn stayed stoic, raising her voice above the din. "Everyone, be quiet now. Make no unnecessary noise. Renwick, take us up."

We'd been hovering below the veil, but now Renwick took the wheel and shouted orders to the sailors, who had gotten themselves under control and seemed glad to have something to do. No one else spoke as the ship rose into the clouds and then came out on the other side. Quynn moved to the railing, keeping her eyes on the sky as if she could see something no one else could. Below us, the veil was thick but calm, a white blanket.

"Pull the sails," Quynn ordered.

Renwick repeated it, and the sailors hurried to obey.

"Why are you pulling the sails?" I moved to stand beside her, my hand wrapped tight around the still-cold rock. "Without the sails, we won't be able to escape our pursuers."

Quynn narrowed her eyes at me. "Was I not clear? No unnecessary noise. That includes your incessant gabbing."

I pressed my lips together, remembering what Arun had said about her. I rather wanted to keep my head on my neck, after all, so I stepped aside, running smack into Arun, who was standing surprisingly close. He steadied me with a hand on my back, a hand that he left there.

I was about to say something to him—probably something pointless and inane—when there was a sound like nothing I had ever heard. A single high-pitched note, a song that wrapped around me and held me in place. Not quite a human's voice, nor a bird's call, nor the blast of a horn. Something entirely new and different. Something beautiful and haunting.

"Here they come," the captain whispered.

I drew my ax, ready to face whatever it was.

And then the clouds moved, and a monster rolled out of them. It had the streamlined shape of a fish with a thin, long fin on its back trailing behind it and paddle-like arms on each side. It breached the clouds like a fish surfacing, first its face, then its back, and then its finned tail, slapping the clouds and parting them briefly before it disappeared beneath us. Without thinking, I followed the crowd to the other side of the ship where we watched it surface again. This time, it stuck its elongated head straight up out of the clouds, snapped a bird out of the air with its giant mouth, and then fell back, emitting another high-pitched wail that was answered by a dozen more somewhere around us.

Beside me, Estrid gasped, her sword in her hand.

"Put away your weapons," Quynn scolded us. She was behind the wheel again, maneuvering the ship to drop it into the clouds.

We obeyed, even though it felt unnatural to face this threat without something to use to defend ourselves. As soon as I dropped the ax into my belt, I felt fingers wrap around my own. I looked over to see Arun smiling at me. He didn't let go.

"Aren't they beautiful?"

"What are they?" I asked.

"Sky whales. A whole pod of them."

I'd heard of whales but never seen them, in the sky or in the water. Quynn had dropped us into the veil so that the whales were enormous shadows all around us. One came so close that its fin floated over the edge of the ship. I reached up with my free hand and let it float over my fingers.

"It's so soft," I whispered.

The whale called back its response, a lower tone that vibrated the ship beneath my feet.

Arun laughed and squeezed my hand.

On the bow of the ship, a smaller whale faced off against Stiarna, floating just out of her reach but studying her with a large black eye. She stretched her neck out, inching carefully to the edge of the bowsprit until her beak brushed the whale's dark blue hide. The whale startled and flipped away, the wind from its tail sending the ship into a spin. Quynn called out a quiet order and righted the ship with the help of her crew, holding the *Wind Wraith* steady as the pod of whales passed us.

"I thought we would be in danger," I said, my eyes still on the creature's shadows, even as they grew smaller and more distant.

"Danger can come in any form." Arun let go of my hand and

patted me on the head, making me wince. "Fighting isn't always the answer."

With the sky whales gone, Quynn took us back above the veil. The sun had turned the sky golden-yellow. Plateaus poked out of the veil in the distance, none of them close enough to see clearly.

The captain looked down at me from the helm, her hands on the wooden steering wheel. "Now, D'ahvol, where to?"

CHAPTER 11

At the wayfinder's stone's behest, we flew in circles for the next two days.

Everyone was mad at me.

I was mad at the rock.

Every time I looked at it, it said the same thing. And every time I had to report it to the captain, she looked at me with such contempt that I felt like I shrank a bit. Soon, I would be the world's smallest D'ahvol.

The stone kept us over Bruhier, directing us east until we hit the coast, south for half a day, then back inland for a while before turning us gradually north and starting over again. Was it lost? Were we missing something? On the second pass, Quynn took us below the veil to see if there was something there, but it was only the same thick, dangerous jungle. After a blazetaur swung its poisonous barbed tail at us, she took us back up above the clouds. If we were going to fly in circles, at least she would keep us safe.

Estrid wouldn't talk to me or hardly even look at me. I didn't know how long she would continue to blame me for Erik's absence, but it didn't seem that there was anything I could do to convince her it wasn't my fault. She'd relied on him and followed him for so long that she seemed about as aimless as the wayfinder's stone without him there. Even I had to admit it was strange to see her by herself.

Arun, on the other hand, became my constant companion. He was the only one, it seemed, not annoyed by me. We sat together on the deck whenever there was nothing else to do, and stayed up late into the night, wooing each other with tales of our respective homes. He asked me constant questions about Bor'sur, my hometown in the Western March, and about the Ahvoli traditions. I told him about Yule, which we celebrated on the winter solstice, and the Midsummer feast on the summer solstice.

"I cannot wait to see it," he'd said dreamily, as if it were a given that he would be invited.

I decided that if we ever got out of this, I would take him home with me. It was almost impossible to imagine introducing him to my father—a gentry elf and a D'ahvol warrior. But then again, that was what we were, wasn't it? And we got along just fine. I thought my father would, too, once he got over his initial shock.

Finally, on the third day, when we should have turned south, the stone instead directed us inland, toward a distant plateau that we'd seen in passing but never approached.

"What is it?" I asked, standing at the helm sandwiched between Quynn and Arun.

"I think it's Morasera," Quynn answered. "An elven city of scholars."

This city was not as flashy as Lamruil or as run-down as Fairlow, but somewhere in between, with wooden houses built high in the trees and lit by suspended yooperlite stones shining yellow in the twilight. It wasn't until we'd gotten closer, though, that I saw maybe why the stone was bringing us to this plateau.

It was under attack.

I ran to the edge of the ship and leaned over to get a better view, hanging onto the rigging for support. The elves were fighting back familiar dark shapes—ur'gels. Thankfully, these ur'gels didn't seem to be of the flying variety. These elves, though, were obviously not fighters. Quynn had called them scholars, and it showed. They used staffs and walking sticks. As I watched, an ur'gel grabbed one elf, hoisted him up, and tossed him over the edge of the plateau. Stiarna took off after him, wings tucked against her sides as she dove.

"Take us down," I said to Quynn, forgetting that she didn't like to be ordered around.

She raised one cocky eyebrow at me. "I'll take you and your friends down, but I'm not leaving the *Wraith*. No ur'gel will get its nasty claws on my ship."

I shook my head. "Fine, whatever. Just hurry."

Surprisingly, she did, hovering just over the ground while Estrid, Arun, and I scrambled down using the hull nets. When an ur'gel approached us, one of the crew felled it with an arrow through its chest.

"We'll cover you from here," the crewman called to us.

I nodded my thanks at him and threw myself into the melee.

There was something satisfying about killing an ur'gel. They were so stupid and so brutal that it felt like giving them a taste of their own medicine. With my ax and my sword, I could take out two of them in just a few swings, even without Estrid watching my back. I tried to keep an eye on my sister, but she was busy taking her rage out on the monsters, and that was fine with me as long as she didn't get herself killed. At one point, Arun and I fell into the easy, back-to-back fighting style of the D'ahvol. At first it was strange, but it didn't take me long to learn the feel of him. The way our shoulders were almost the exact same width apart. How when his right arm came up to strike, his left hand reached back and grazed my wrist just to keep track of me. Before long, it was as if we'd been fighting like this our entire lives.

The stone burned hot through my pocket against my chest, which told me we were in the right place. But why would the stone, which earlier today had been dead-set against putting me in danger, throw me down on the middle of a plateau rife with the enemy?

An elven man ran by me, pursued by an ur'gel with blue-black skin and a pig's snout, wearing only a loin cloth and a bandoleer. I took a step forward and drove my sword into the monster's back. It jerked to a stop and fell in a pool of black blood. Bracing my foot on its lower back, I pulled the sword out and wiped it on the grass before stepping back against Arun.

Only he wasn't there. I turned around and saw that he'd been surrounded, pulled forward by a horde of ugly, pig-faced ur'gels who were tossing him back and forth. He'd block one's advances only to be pushed into another. One wrong step and he was dead.

I launched myself forward with a battle cry that drew a lot of shocked eyes to me. I killed two ur'gels with one blow. When another one managed to knock me off-balance, I dropped to the ground and opened a wound behind its knees. It howled and fell beside me, where I bashed in its head with the hilt of my sword. I could feel the warm, black blood on my face and hands, but I didn't care. Then Arun was there, pulling me to my feet and wiping his thumbs under my eyes.

"I'm fine, I'm fine," he was saying repeatedly, trying to convince me or himself, I wasn't sure.

Over his shoulder, I saw an elven woman running toward us, her only weapon an iron candlestick that she white-knuckled in one hand. She plowed into Arun, bounced off, and scrambled backward on the ground. Her pursuer, an ur'gel with a more human face than the others, laughed, his lower incisors gleaming where they poked out over his upper lip. I stepped over the woman, swinging my sword around and severing the ur'gel's head with one stroke. That elf on Fairlow really had done an outstanding job sharpening the blade.

Arun helped the woman to her feet and was brushing her off when she looked over at me. Her eyes danced across my soiled clothes and dirty face and landed on the star beside my eye. She lifted a hand and ran her thumb over it before I could move away. Her hand came back black with ur'gel blood.

"Is that—? Are you—?" She gaped open-mouthed at me.

Someone else came up to her, a thin, older man with a walking stick that had been cracked in two. "Agose, are you OK?"

But the woman, Agose, didn't answer. Instead, she pointed at me. "Do you see this?"

The man looked at me for the first time, his thick eyebrows drawn together over light blue eyes. Then he noticed the star. "The heir," he breathed.

"The heir," the woman repeated, her voice louder.

The shout echoed through the city as the fighting stopped. In the silence, a battle cry rang out from the ur'gels, who had turned their attention to me. "The heir!" one of them cried in a deep, husky voice. "Get her!"

It was Estrid who silenced him with a blow to the back of the head, but it was too late.

They were coming for me.

CHAPTER 12

The three of us turned and ran. The elves of Morasera were little help, but when we got close enough, arrows from the archers on the *Wind Wraith* sailed over our heads and kept a lot of the ur'gels at bay. As soon as we were on the hull nets, Quynn took the ship off the ground, not even waiting for us to get on the deck. Luckily, we got over the railing without any difficulty, collapsing on the wooden slats with relief. Stiarna was already there, perched overhead on a yardarm.

"I knew that was a bad idea," the captain said, scowling down at where the three of us sat in a pool of black ur'gel blood.

"It's not like we had much of a choice." I pushed myself to my feet and turned to help Estrid, but she ignored my outstretched hand. Still mad, I guessed. "Although I don't know why the stone would lead us to danger."

Renwick, who seemed to have the most experience with wayfinder's stones, said, "The magic of the stone is that it always knows what it's doing. Unfortunately, the bearer of the stone is not always privy to its plan."

There it was again—magic. Even though I was supposed to

repel it by the very nature of my race, I seemed to attract it at every turn. I both hated it and depended on it. The stone wasn't giving us any clues now, so Quynn made the decision to stop on another plateau for supplies.

Ereshys was similar to Lamruil in its extravagance. It was a series of domed structures that crisscrossed a river running across the plateau, culminating in a waterfall that dropped out of sight beneath the veil. That's where the market was, on bridges that were suspended over the waterfall. Quynn brought the *Wind Wraith* into a slip on the south side and we disembarked. Even Quynn actually got off of the ship, tossing an attendant a gold coin to keep an eye on her.

"There's another one in it for you if she's untouched when I get back."

The attendant, a boy of maybe ten, nodded and posted himself beside the *Wraith*, arms crossed behind his back. If he knew a griffin was on board, I bet he wouldn't be so quick to turn his back on the ship. But I kept that fact to myself as we headed down the dock and entered the busy market.

I took our blades to get sharpened—appreciating the elven skill with weapons after last time—while Estrid, Arun, and the crew retrieved food and water. Estrid was also charged with bringing back an extra set of clothes for the two of us. I could only hope she didn't bring me something ridiculous, like a skirt, as revenge for leaving Erik.

I was wearing a hat pulled low over my head to hide the star mark when I got in line at the blade smith's booth. There were a couple of elves in front of me, but neither even glanced in my direction. Their conversation, though, caught my attention.

"—ur'gels."

"Ur'gels? Ur'gels aren't real." This from a younger man, barely older than I was.

His companion, an older elven gentleman with silver hair, shrugged. "Well, something destroyed Ulenqua and Erelon."

"A monster. Maybe a flock of dreadwings."

"I'm telling you, Finetu, it was ur'gels. And they're looking for the Suun heir."

The younger man—Finetu—laughed. "What, am I living in a child's story book? This is insane. You can't tell me you believe in that."

Someone else chimed in, a woman who had come in behind me. She leaned around me and said, "My cousin was in Erelon when they came."

"When who came?" asked Finetu.

I ducked my head low but couldn't hide my interest in the conversation.

The woman glanced at me, then back at the men. "The ur'gels."

"Impossible," Finetu insisted.

She persisted. "The whole city was destroyed, burnt to the ground. Men, women, children. All of them, dead. It didn't matter if they surrendered or not. My cousin was on the only airship that got out of port before the fires."

The older man shook his head, smiling grimly. "I'm telling you," he said again. "Something bad is coming. I can feel it. We can only hope that Onen Suun's heir will come to our rescue."

I shivered, the tremor starting in my core and spreading to my shoulders.

The line moved forward, and the men turned around. The woman looked at me. "Do you believe it?"

Nodding, I said, "I saw them on Morasera today."

She gasped. "Today?"

"This morning."

"Onen save us."

She had no idea.

I excused myself and stepped out of line, hurrying back through the crowd. I searched for familiar faces and saw none. Not Estrid, Arun, Quynn, or even Renwick. My panic grew, and my mind raced. The ur'gels were looking for me, and everyone knew it. What would the elves do if they discovered me in their midst? Offer me up to the monsters on a silver platter? Or maybe they would try to protect me, as I had tried to protect the people on Morasera. Would the elves on Morasera spread news of my appearance and let others know I was helping them? To make matters worse, both the elves and the ur'gels had seen me leave on the *Wind Wraith*. They knew who I was with and what I looked like. It was fine when I was pretending to be the heir for the ur'gels, but if the elves started holding me up as the Suun heir…

This could be bad for everyone, not just for me.

I ran into Quynn at a stand that sold fruits and vegetables where she was haggling with the vendor over the price of a bag of tomatoes. I made sure the hat was covering my mark and grabbed her arm.

"We should probably go," I said through gritted teeth.

She looked at me, raised her eyebrows at the hat, and then turned back to the vendor. "That's my final offer."

The man shook his head. "Fine."

She counted out her coins and dropped them into the man's hand. He handed her the bag and she slung it over her shoulder, pulling me away.

"Have you heard the talk?" I asked, not able to stand her silence.

"Yes."

"They're looking for me."

"They've always been looking for you, if I understand correctly. The ur'gels are just increasing their efforts, as it were. You told the king this would happen." She crossed the street to another booth and purchased a five-pound bag of jerked meat while I stood nervously behind her, avoiding eye contact. I was sure my efforts to look casual only made me look more suspicious.

"Should I get another ship? Separate myself from the *Wind Wraith*? To throw them off the track."

"Sure," Quynn said with a casual shrug, "if you want to die."

I stopped walking, stunned, as she continued to move away. Taking a couple of strides to catch up, I said to her, "Of course, I don't want to die. That's the whole point."

"Then you stay with me. I'm the best captain in the air."

"I might have to disagree with that," came Arun's voice over my shoulder. Large sacks of potatoes and cornmeal slung over his shoulders. He eyed Quynn's smaller parcels. "Or, if nothing else, I'm certainly a better negotiator than you."

Quynn made a small noise of dissent and continued her charge through the crowd. Behind her back, Arun slipped something wrapped in parchment paper into my hand.

"What is it?" I whispered to him.

When he answered, his face was close enough to mine that I could smell the sweetness of his breath. "Penydes." He opened his mouth to show me the hard candy braced between his front teeth. "Try it. I used to love this as a boy. My mother told me it would rot my teeth and made me scrub my mouth whenever she caught me with one."

I unwrapped the small package and popped the hard candy in my mouth. At first, the sugary sweetness was almost too much, but then it began to dissolve and soften. I widened my eyes and looked over to find him smiling at me expectantly. For just that one moment, it was like we were just a boy and a girl. Not an elf and a D'ahvol. Not a champion of lost causes and a savior of the world. I could have kissed him. I knew exactly what he would taste like.

But then Quynn snapped her fingers and broke the spell. I tucked the candy into my cheek and hurried after her, Arun at my heels. We kept our eyes open for Estrid but reached the dock without seeing her.

Quynn flipped the attendant another coin and held her arm out at the ship. "All aboard."

"We have to wait for Estrid," I objected.

The captain did not even look back at me as she boarded her ship. "No, we don't. You were the one who wanted to get out of here. Now, let's go."

"Not without my sister." I had to raise my voice to be sure she heard me, but she gave no indication she had. To Arun, who was still beside me, I repeated it. "I can't leave without my sister."

A hand clapped against my shoulder and I whirled around to find Estrid there. "That would be a first," she said, stepping past me, and walking up the gangplank to board the ship, leaving me staring after her, my heart a lump in my throat.

CHAPTER 13

I was glad when night came and shrouded the ship in darkness. It felt like I could, at least temporarily, let my guard down. In the dark, the *Wind Wraith* was indistinguishable from any other ship in the sky. Aupra was dull and distant, and Gleet was low on the southern horizon, a blue glow that helped us orient ourselves but didn't provide much more light than that. Not for the first time, I marveled at how Quynn did what she did with such unwavering confidence. At exactly how much constant practice and blind luck it took to keep an airship aloft.

One good thing about the darkness of the sky was that it let the stars come out in vast numbers, hundreds of thousands of them poking holes in the blackness. I leaned against the railing and searched for shapes in the stars: faces, and words, and great warriors wielding swords, and princesses with crowns on their heads.

After a while, footsteps warned me of someone's presence.

"That's a lot of D'ahvol." It was Arun. He leaned on the railing beside me, our arms touching.

I pushed off the railing and turned around, looking over at him. "Where have you been?"

"Below deck. Your sister came down, though, so I got out of there."

"Was she okay?"

He nodded. "Going to bed, I think."

It was late, and most of the crew was in bed, too. Only the captain was on deck, standing at the helm behind us. Except for the occasional breeze whipping a sail taut, it was mostly quiet. Almost uncomfortably so.

"What about you?" Arun asked. "Are you all right?"

I chuckled, but I was sure he could tell there was no humor in the sound. "Everything is just so … different. So much harder than I ever thought it would be. I'm different." I had always been the little warrior girl, my siblings' shadow, their protector when they thought they didn't need one. Now I was the one putting them in danger, dragging them into this hunt for the heir and pitting them against ur'gels and empaths. Leaving Erik behind with the knowledge he would likely come under fire. Estrid was right. I was changing. And I wasn't sure I liked it.

But Arun just shrugged. "That's life, though, isn't it? Circumstances change, and people change to adapt to them. You didn't make Dag'draath do what he did. You didn't ask the Sisters to transfer the mark to you. You're doing what you have to do to survive."

"Not really." I tilted my head back and closed my eyes, unable to look at him. "If all I wanted was to survive, then I could just take my family and hide away in the Western March somewhere, pretend none of this was happening. It would take a long time for any of it to reach us there. We could probably live out the rest of our lives in peace."

"Is that what you want, though?"

"What?"

"Is that what you want?" Arun grabbed both of my wrists and

pulled me to him. My eyes opened and I was looking at him instead of the night sky. At his wide, dark eyes and furrowed brow. "To hide and spend the rest of your life in peace while the world burns around you?"

"No. No, of course not." I shook my head and dropped my eyes.

"Of course not," he said in a quieter voice. "And thank Onen, because what would we do without you?"

This time when I laughed, I meant it. "I'm sure you could find some other lost cause to champion."

One corner of his mouth quirked up and he let go of my wrists, though he didn't take a step back. "You're not a lost cause." When he talked, I heard something in his mouth clank against his teeth.

"Young man, is that a candy in your mouth?" I teased.

He smiled and bared his teeth, showing the pale disc clamped between his front teeth.

The sight of it made my mouth water. "I hate that you gave me one," I said wistfully. "Now, I'll forever crave another."

"You can have this one." He spoke around the candy, not making any move to give it to me.

I realized I was staring at his mouth, so I raised my eyes to meet his.

"Here." He leaned forward.

Before I could second-guess myself or run away, I pushed up onto my toes. My eyes were open when my teeth collided with his and I saw his face change from shock to pleasure. And then it wasn't our teeth but our lips brushing tentatively together, and his tongue slipped the candy into my mouth which exploded with the sugary sweetness. His hands snaked around my hips and pulled me against him just as I pushed him away, my hands on his chest.

"Thanks," I said around the candy, giving it a satisfying

crunch. I was going for casual, but I wondered if he could feel my heart racing against him.

He groaned and leaned his forehead against mine. When I tried to step away, he tightened his grip. "Where are you going?"

"Arun, I—" I choked on the words I knew I had to say, but I cleared my throat and forced them out, my eyes on my boots. "Arun, I can't do this. I can't endanger you, too."

His hands shifted, balling my vest up in his fists. "What are you talking about?"

"I'll always have this target on my back. On my face." I touched the mark beside my eye.

"I don't care about that. Do you think I care about that?"

"I think you should. I'm so tired of hurting the people I … care about."

He ducked down and stuck his face under mine, forcing me to look at him. "There's only one thing that I ask. You have to promise me something."

I wanted to object. Tell him no, I wasn't in the position to make anyone any promises. I didn't even want this, to feel like this about him. It would only lead to heartache. But I pressed my lips together and waited.

Arun smiled. "Take me with you wherever you go. I'll keep you in a lifetime supply of Penydes if you just promise not to leave me behind."

In spite of myself, I smiled. It was an offer I just couldn't refuse. I slid my hands up to his shoulders. "Fine," I said through gritted teeth, "but I'm going to hold you to that."

His lips touched mine, feather-light and questioning.

"Hey, lovebirds," Quynn said, her voice echoing in the silent night. "You're blocking my view."

I jerked away from him and ducked my head, turning my back on her, crunching the last bits of the candy between my teeth.

But Arun looked right at the captain, a grin on his handsome face. "Of what? The darkness?"

"Of anything but you two sucking face," she called back, but I could hear the teasing smile on her lips.

"Feel free to look away." With that, Arun put a hand on the small of my back and pressed me against him, bringing his mouth down on mine again. His earlier hesitancy was gone. This wasn't a kiss that asked, but a kiss that demanded, and I gave it to him. Breathless, excited, and uncertain. And terrified.

But I was a Svand. And Svands faced their fears with their eyes wide open, ready for whatever would come next.

CHAPTER 14

Ahorn blasted through the stillness of the next morning, jerking me from sleep. Arun and I were lying side-by-side on the deck, my head nestled against his shoulder and his arm wrapped around me. We'd spent the night like that, neither one of us wanting to break the spell by going below deck and facing Estrid. But we regretted it now. The crew surged up to the deck, pounding feet nearly trampling us.

"Hey, watch it," Arun told one man who tripped over my leg.

"What are you doing?" the sailor asked with a scowl, righting himself. "Didn't you hear the horn? Get up." And he ran away.

Embarrassed, I pushed myself to sitting and rubbed the sleep from my eyes. "I heard it. What was it?"

"A call for all hands on deck," Arun answered. He stood and reached a hand down for me.

I let him pull me up and then tried to casually drop his hand while I pretended to brush dust from my clothes. I knew things would look different in the light of day, and I didn't want him to think I held him to anything he said last night.

Arun saw through my act, though. He snatched my hand back up and pressed my fingers to his lips. Then he squeezed my hand and looked at me intently. "Don't be weird, okay?"

I took a deep breath. "Okay."

"Or I'll have to sweep you off your feet in front of all these sailors."

When I grimaced, he laughed and finally let me go.

At the helm, Quynn was barking orders.

"What's going on?" Arun asked.

"That." She pointed straight ahead.

We turned and followed the direction of her finger, our eyes landing on a black cloud of birds.

No, not birds.

"Ur'gels," Arun said with a sigh.

Quynn looked back and forth between Arun and me and must have been able to see the defeat on our faces. "What did I tell you yesterday?" she asked me.

"To stay with you. That you're the best airship captain."

"Right." She shouted something to a passing sailor. Then, to me, "Do what I say, and we'll be fine."

I nodded my agreement. Even Arun, who didn't like taking orders from her, was silent, listening.

"Draw your weapons and fight, but when I say hang on, you hang on. Got it?"

"Got it," we said in unison.

Estrid appeared then, her hair still messy from sleep. "Got what?"

We filled her in as we made our way to the bow of the ship, stepping over ropes and weapons and the legs of men who were crawling around on the ground, tying things down. She was still standoffish, but she seemed to have cooled down some. At least, she wasn't openly insulting me, so there was that. I still let Arun do most of the talking.

"Hang on?" Estrid looked like she'd woken up and stepped into a nightmare. A fight, the Svand sisters could handle. A fight in the air where we were told to "hang on" and crew members were anchoring themselves to the ship with ropes? That was something we were less prepared for.

We didn't have time to back out, though. The ur'gels were on us like a swarm of bees, but the sailors were ready for them. Renwick was the one I noticed first, probably because he was the highest. He leapt from the mainmast as if he had wings. The rope wrapped around his wrist pulled taut and swung him around. He grabbed one ur'gel by the wing and slung it to the deck, where it landed at my feet. I hadn't even pulled my ax yet, so I stomped on its back and jerked its wing, snapping it before Estrid and I tossed the body overboard. The ur'gel, still stunned, made no move to save himself.

That was how it went on for the first few minutes—one of the *Wind Wraith's* crew would sail out into the open sky, knock an ur'gel down to us, and we would dispatch it. I kept my eyes open for Savarah, ready to pull out the locket and use it to finally beat her once and for all, but she was nowhere to be seen.

Even without her, the ur'gels kept coming. There were so many that they started getting past the sailors, landing on the deck and tucking in their wings, drawing their weapons and charging at us. With every one I killed, another took its place. I heard a shout and looked up in time to see an ur'gel cut through a rope and send one of our men—Renwick, I realized when I saw the flash of gold in his hair—plummeting to the ground.

"Stiarna!" I cried. Together, the griffin and I leapt from the railing.

I heard Arun say, "Frida, don't," and I felt fingers graze the back of my shirt, but I didn't pause. I couldn't pause, or Renwick would be lost.

I kept my hand on Stiarna's shoulder but didn't get my legs

around her until we were already in the air, diving after Renwick. My ax was in my hand and I swung at every ur'gel we passed, but it didn't take long for us to drop below the fight. We caught up to Renwick as we entered the veil. When he saw us, his eyes went wide with shock, but then he tucked his legs in and rolled so that he was face-down and could reach for us. But I didn't want his hands. I had my eye on the rope still tied around his wrist. It was closer to me, an easier target as it fluttered in the wind several yards above his head.

Tucking my ax away, I leaned over, one hand wrapped in the feathers at the base of Stiarna's neck, the other stretching for the rope. My fingers wrapped around it.

"Hold on," I grunted, not sure if I was talking to Renwick, Stiarna, or myself. Maybe all of us.

Stiarna spread her wings to stop our fall and the rope went taut. It felt like it nearly pulled my shoulder out of its socket. Of course, it was the same shoulder that an ur'gel had speared during the fight in Barepost. It burned, but I held on, grinding my teeth against the pain.

We were finally ascending again, and the ship was directly overhead. The ur'gels were swarming the ship, hanging from the hull nets, and standing on the railings, rocking it like they'd done to the *Iron Duchess* in the Valley of the Horses.

"That's not good," Renwick called up to me.

"Are they going to capsize the ship?"

"Not if the captain can do it first."

I squinted down at him. "Wait, what?"

"You might want to get out of the way."

I nudged Stiarna to the left with my knees and she followed, veering out from beneath the ship but still angling upward. I heard shouts of "hang on," and "what's happening," and suddenly the *Wraith* was tilting precariously toward us. I caught a glimpse of blonde hair—Estrid. She'd tied herself to the mainmast. Then

Arun appeared at the railing, searching the skies. For me, I realized.

"Arun!" I shouted, waving to get his attention. He had to tie himself off or he was going to fall.

But he didn't see me.

The ship kept rolling. The sailors were still fighting, swinging around on their ropes with nothing below them, breaking wings and dropping ur'gels who free fell into the clouds below. Sailors were even standing on the hull as it became the top side, dispatching the surprised ur'gels with an ease I'd never seen before in someone this high up in the air. No one noticed Arun, who was sliding across the wooden slats, hands scrambling for purchase. An ur'gel with a torn wing was next to him and reached out, grabbing Arun's ankle. Arun kicked but the ur'gel didn't let go. They hit the railing together and tumbled over. Stiarna was close enough for me to grab him, but she wouldn't be able to hold all our weight.

"You have to get on board," I shouted to Renwick, who nodded in agreement. With Stiarna's help, I slung Renwick up, letting go of the rope at the very last moment. His hand wrapped around the ship's railing and he held on tight. On my other side, I reached an arm out and caught Arun as he fell, our hands clasping each other's elbows. He kicked again and the ur'gel finally let go, tumbling into the clouds.

I flung him onto Stiarna's back and whipped around to glare at him.

"Thank Onen," he gasped. "I thought you were dead."

Even there, in the air, with ur'gels raining down around us, I needed to make one thing clear. "Just because I kissed you, don't think that I'm going to stop fighting and doing what—"

He shut me up when he covered my mouth with his, our noses squishing together in his eagerness. When he pulled away, he said, "I'm pretty sure I was the one who kissed you."

"What I'm trying to say—"

"I know," he said. "I get it. I don't want you to change. I'm sorry. I was just scared. For you."

An ur'gel spun past us. Stiarna kicked out with one clawed leg and caught it in the side. It screamed as it fell. Overhead, on the upside-down ship, the sailors began their victory cheer.

CHAPTER 15

When the *Wind Wraith* was upright again, Stiarna landed on the crowded deck. We were met by Estrid. She had rope-burn marks around her wrists, but she took the time to look me over and make sure I was okay. It was as close to forgiveness as I figured I would get from her.

The sailors were already working to clean the ur'gel blood with mops and buckets and soapy towels. Renwick, whose life I had just saved, handed me a wooden bucket filled with water and a rag that might once have been white but was now a dull brown color.

I took them from him. "Seriously?"

He shrugged. "No rest for the weary." He turned to walk away, but then seemed to think better of it and turned around. "Thanks, by the way." As if it had been no big deal, keeping him from shattering into smithereens in the Bruhier jungle. He passed two more rags to Estrid and Arun, and then approached Stiarna, who was grooming herself in her favorite spot near the bow of the ship. Instead of forcing her into menial labor, he patted her on the head and gave her a huge fish that she gobbled down greedily.

Ugh.

We scrubbed the deck for hours in spite of our aching muscles. While the sailors, including Arun, joyfully regaled each other with tales of victory or sang bawdy songs, Estrid and I crawled around on our hands and knees and grumbled angrily, cursing Quynn under our breath.

It wasn't until night fell that Renwick collected our supplies and dismissed us. Most of the sailors went below decks for supper. While I usually took my meals on the deck, I followed, starved and tired, ready to eat and go straight to bed. Everyone else was in high spirits, though, even Quynn. The captain raised her glass of ale to me and my sister, who sat at the opposite end of the table from her with Arun.

"To the D'ahvol," she said. "The second-best fighters in the air."

"To the D'ahvol," chorused her crew.

Estrid and I flushed, hiding our pink cheeks behind our glasses of ale. The drink was strong and burned going down, but the more I drank, the easier it became to swallow and the better the food tasted.

As soon as supper was over, the empty plates were cleared and cups were filled with ale, Quynn brought out a deck of cards.

Estrid's eyes lit up.

Quynn noticed. "We don't play often," she said, shuffling the cards expertly in her long-fingered hands, "but we enjoy a good game now and then. Can I deal you in?"

Without answering, Estrid scooted out a chair and sat back down.

Then, Quynn noticed me still standing. "And you?"

"No." I waved my hands in front of me. "No, I'd be no good. I can hardly keep my eyes open."

Arun was behind me, standing too close. I didn't know if the heat in my neck was from the drink or his proximity. I wondered if he would stay.

But before he could say anything, Quynn eyed him over my shoulder and said, "Don't even think about it, Phina."

If he hadn't been thinking about it, he was now. "What?"

"You're not invited to our game. I know all about you." She began to deal, flipping the cards quickly to the group around her.

Arun crossed his arms over his chest. "What do you know about me?"

"That you're a cheater."

The card players murmured to each other and gave him narrow looks.

I stepped back to get a good look at him and his reaction.

He seemed adequately shocked, his mouth open and his brow furrowed. "That's ludicrous. I'm no cheater. And how would you know? You've never played a game with me in your life."

Quynn stacked the remaining cards on the table and peeked at her own hand. "Maybe not, but my brother has."

"Your brother?" The confusion on his face was as real as the shock.

The satisfied look on Quynn's face told me that this—whatever Arun had done to her brother—was the real reason she gave Arun a tough time. "Have you ever heard of the Wynleth family?" she asked Arun.

Arun shook his head.

"No, you wouldn't have. The Phinas and the Wynleths don't exactly run in the same circles. The Wynleths come from nothing and have nothing. My father, though, worked his way up through the ranks to become a master airship builder. We had a small but decent life, but when he and my mother died, all they had to leave us were the two airships still in the Wynleth name. The *Wind Wraith* and one other."

"The *Iron Duchess*." Arun uncrossed his arms and stared at the captain.

"Yes," Quynn confirmed. The card players were making their bets, but Quynn folded her hand and leaned back. "The ship that you stole from him."

He held up a finger. "To be fair, I won it. He wagered it and he lost it."

"You cheated. My brother never loses."

"I didn't cheat."

"The airship was all he had left of our parents. You could have shown mercy."

Arun shook his head. "You would respect me even less if I had."

I left them to continue their argument and went to our small sleeping quarters, where I took off my leather armor and washed up, then lay in my cot, studying the wayfinder's stone, which had been curiously quiet today. It was still not giving off any clues, so I tucked it under my pillow beside the compass and the locket and rolled over, closing my eyes in the darkness.

Sometime later, a small, shuffling sound woke me. The cot across from me creaked, and there was a tired sigh. I knew without looking that it was Arun, and the lack of snoring from the cot above me told me Estrid was still at the card game. I waited until Arun lay down and his breathing grew even, and then I slid out of my cot, as quiet as a hunter stalking its prey. There's no way to get into a cot quietly, though, and Arun jolted awake as his cot creaked and moaned under my weight.

"It's just me," I whispered to him.

"Hello, just me." He held an arm up and I slipped in, pressing my back against his chest. With the extra weight, the sides of the cot folded up around us, creating our own little cocoon. He buried his face against my neck, where my hair was getting too long, and breathed deeply.

"Don't do that, I stink."

"It's that irresistible scent of ur'gel blood."

I swatted at him and he chuckled quietly, pressing me closer. I'd been nervous about crawling into his cot—all joking aside, it was the first time I'd made the first move. But I wanted to be open to him. I wanted him to know I wanted to be near him. And I was glad I had. It felt right, to be tucked up against him in the dark.

When I had about drifted back to sleep, Arun asked, "Do you ever wonder what the heir is like?"

I came slowly back to awareness, so it took me a second to process his question, and another second to realize that for all the searching for her and talking about her, I had never actually thought of her as a real person. "Well, I guess I thought she would be like me."

"Like you?"

"Strong. A fighter. Training her whole life to be a warrior and fight Dag'draath."

Arun grunted. I felt it against my back, a low grumble.

"What? You don't think so?"

"Remember we promised Ravyn that we would help her? So … maybe not."

"Why would they hide her away if not to prepare her for what was to come?"

This time, I felt him shrug. "I could be wrong."

I could only hope he was.

Sleep came easily after that. So easily, in fact, that I didn't hear Estrid come in. It wasn't until she was screaming at me I finally rose to consciousness, peeling myself away from Arun and sitting up on the edge of his cot.

"What in Onen's name are you doing?" she shrieked.

"What are you talking about?" I rubbed my eyes. "What time is it?"

Arun shifted behind me but couldn't sit without rolling me out onto the floor, so he just lay there, looking up at Estrid with wide eyes.

Estrid drew her sword and suddenly the room got even smaller. "I'll kill you, elf." He was demoted back to "elf" now.

I stood quickly.

The cot shifted and dumped Arun onto the floor against the wall. Estrid stabbed at him and tore the thick material of the bed. He flattened himself against the wall and shuffled away from her, staying just out of her reach.

I grabbed Estrid's shoulder, but she shook me off. Her sword took a chunk out of the wall and for all that I didn't want to be on the other end of it, I also didn't want to face Quynn's wrath if we destroyed any part of her ship.

"Estrid, stop," I hissed, stepping between her and Arun. "He didn't do anything."

When she finally focused on me, her cheeks were flushed red. "Didn't do anything? What was he doing in your bed?"

"I was in *his* bed."

She paused, looked back and forth between my cot and Arun's, realization dawning on her face. "You … you...," Estrid collapsed onto my cot.

I looked at Arun, who had gone completely still, prey afraid to remind the predator it was still there. "Can you give us a minute?"

He nodded and left without looking at my sister, closing the thin wooden door behind him. I was sure it was too late for privacy, though. The whole ship had to have heard Estrid's blow-up.

She didn't look up at me when she spoke. Her voice was so low I wasn't even sure I was meant to hear her, but I did. "I'm supposed to protect you from this."

"I don't need to be protected from Arun," I said, willing her to look at me, to look up and *see* me.

As if she didn't hear me, she went on. "I'm the only one left who can keep you safe. You and Erik go around fulfilling your own destinies, doing whatever you want to do, and I'm left chasing you around, trying to save you from yourselves. And now ... now it's just you and me. And Arun, I guess. What are you doing with him?"

"I just ... I'm..." It was hard to answer her when I didn't have an answer for myself. "I'm giving him a chance. Giving myself a chance to ... to let someone in."

"I can't protect you from things you walk into willingly. I can't..."

"I don't need to be protected," I said again. "I need..." I sat down beside her, the cot sinking below my weight and pushing us together. "I need to be loved. Not by him. By you. I need you to love me. That's all. Love me and accept me for who I am." I was rambling. I reached under my pillow and pulled out the wayfinder's stone and brandished it at her as if my identity were bound to it. "The non-heir. The maybe savior of the world who has no idea what she's doing most of the time. Just love me. Frida Svand."

When I worked up the nerve to look at her again, she was staring up at me, speechless for once.

Then, suddenly, my hand was on fire.

I dropped the stone. It clattered to the floor and we both stared down at it while I rubbed my aching palm on the smooth material of my trousers. The room, which had been mostly dark, was now filled with a yellow light as the whole stone blazed.

"What is it doing?" Estrid asked.

The stone wasn't pointing in any particular direction, which led me to believe we were already where we were supposed to be. How long had it been doing this, hidden under my pillow? I felt the strange need to apologize to it before remembering I hated magic and it was a stone. "I think we need to land."

We put our argument to the side, and she went to the deck while I hurriedly dressed. When I came up, the ship was already dropping below the veil. The sailors were quiet for the most part, lining the railing, weapons in hand, as if expecting an attack. Even Stiarna was pacing and nervous. I joined Estrid on the starboard side and looked out. The Bruhier jungle had cleared and we were above a vast brown grassland dotted with flat-topped trees. The only thing that moved was the breeze rustling the grasses. I'd never seen anything like it. Not in the Western March and not on Bruhier.

Quynn put the *Wind Wraith* down and her crew hurried to lower the gangplank. She handed me a curved horn. "I'm not leaving my ship here. You do what you need to do and blow the horn when you're ready to leave. Good luck."

Estrid, Arun, and I disembarked with Stiarna at our heels. The grasses were so high that the tops brushed my thighs and nearly covered Stiarna, who stretched her neck high to be able to see. I didn't like it. Somehow, the quiet grasses were worse than the jungle, which at least offered somewhere to hide from its horrors.

I turned and watched the *Wind Wraith* disappear into the veil, all the while turning the horn over in my hands and contemplating just using it now. Only the stone burning a hole in my vest pocket kept me there until Estrid clapped a hand down on my shoulder and took the horn from me, sliding it into a hook on her belt. It was as if she knew how tempted I was to call Quynn back.

"Well, Frida Svand, where to now?"

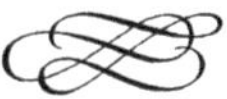

CHAPTER 16

Where to. That was the golden question, wasn't it?

I drew the stone from my pocket to see if it would tell us. When I placed it in my hand beside the compass, the left side began to glow. We walked west, stepping carefully through the high grass, and the faint glow of the sun through the veil cast tall shadows ahead of us. A few yards ahead of us, something rustled in the tall grass. I froze and Arun plowed into my back. I hissed at him to be quiet even though he hadn't said a word and waited. Finally, a long-legged creature with big eyes and fur the same color as the grass came into view, picking its way along. Spotting us, it froze, nose twitching, and then bounded away. Delighted, Stiarna took off after it. Soon, the only thing visible was the tawny tops of her curved wings.

With small, breathy laughs, we continued forward. When nothing else jumped out at us, I began to relax. With no ur'gels and no monsters in sight we seemed to be okay, at least for now. I couldn't forget what Xalph had told me though, that Bruhier was a tricky place. Even if I was relaxed, I couldn't let my guard down, not for an instant.

After a few minutes, Arun fell into step beside me.

"Do you think she's here?" he asked.

Wind rustled my bangs and I brushed my hair back from my face while I decided how to answer him. Finally, I went with a simple, "Yes." I didn't know how to explain it to him beyond that. There was a feeling, a thickness to the air, a tightness in my chest, which told me she was close. Ravyn had told me we were bound to each other, and I hadn't believed her then. But I felt it now, like a thread tying the two of us together. Fate, maybe. I could just imagine Foregin, the god of fate, looking down at us and laughing, tugging me ever closer.

To avoid explaining any of that to Arun, I paused and pulled out the compass and the stone. It wanted us to keep going west.

The sun was nearly above us when the veil thickened, and the grasslands grew dark. Rain fell in thick, heavy droplets. We took shelter under a flat-topped tree and waited for the storm to pass.

"Something feels wrong, doesn't it?" Estrid said, peering up at the clouds. She was pacing back and forth beneath the tree's thin canopy, her shoulders dark with raindrops.

I nodded. "It's too easy. It feels like a trap." I said what I'd been too afraid to even think: "What if we're too late?"

"We're not." Arun shook his head. "You can't think like that."

The rain finally stopped, and we pushed forward, emerging from beneath the tree and crossing a muddy creek that didn't come up past my ankles. I scrambled up the opposite bank, and when I reached the top, I felt … something. Looking over, I saw Estrid shiver and brush at her skin, as if fighting off invisible insects. My own skin was tingling. Beside me, Arun showed me his arm. The hair there was standing on end.

There was a splashing sound behind us, and I turned to see Stiarna coming through the creek. When she got a few feet from us, she jumped back as if something had shocked her.

"Come on," I told her, patting my leg.

She took a tentative step forward but gave a sharp cry and retreated back into the water.

"What is it?" I asked as if expecting her to be able to answer me.

She didn't try to cross again, but raised her beak to the air, the feathers at the nape of her neck standing on end, just like the hair on Arun's arms.

Estrid drew her sword. There was a buzzing sound and she was knocked backward by some invisible force, dropping the sword.

I rushed to her side, pulling her up. "What happened?"

"I was … I was zapped." She brushed herself off and stared down at her sword, unwilling to pick it up.

"Zapped?"

"Like," she grabbed my arm and dug her nails into it, then shook me. "Bzzt!"

"Bzzt?"

She narrowed her eyes. "Yes, bzzt."

"A protection spell," Arun offered. He was standing completely still, his own weapons still sheathed. "It's why Estrid couldn't draw her weapon. And why Stiarna couldn't cross the creek. It must be the boundary of the spell."

"Is that what's crawling all over me?" Estrid asked, rubbing her hands up and down her arms.

He nodded. "It's very strong magic."

Extraordinarily strong magic, used to protect a particularly important person, I suspected. We were getting close.

I told Stiarna to wait for us and then gestured for Arun and Estrid to follow me.

Estrid elbowed her way to the front. "Let me go first."

I put a hand on her arm. "I told you, I don't need protecting."

She smiled. "Maybe not. Maybe it's that I need to protect you."

We moved away from the muddy banks of the creek,

through the sparse trees surrounding it, and back into the dry grasses.

"Look," Estrid said, pointing ahead of us.

I stepped around her and that was when I saw it, a small stone house rising out of the grasslands, its thatched roof the same color as the surrounding grass, which I was sure made it invisible from above. This had to be it—where the heir was hiding. My first instinct was to run for the door but Estrid held me back, forcing me back behind her as she took one painfully slow step after another. I understood. I didn't want to get zapped either, but I wanted this to be over sooner rather than later.

There was a short wooden fence surrounding a well-tended garden. It was difficult to grow anything beneath the veil, so I suspected magic had a hand in this, as well. The gate creaked open and we walked up the flagstone path to the door. When Estrid knocked on it, the door creaked open. It hadn't been latched.

"That's not a good sign," Estrid mumbled to us. Then, to the empty house beyond the door, "Hello?"

No one answered.

"Do we go in?" I asked.

"Not much of a choice," Arun answered.

"I'll go first," Estrid said, narrowing her eyes at me when it looked like I was going to argue. She pushed the door wider, its hinges squeaking, and we followed her inside.

Inside was completely dark. I opened my hand that held the wayfinder's stone and held it flat in my hand, thinking it could provide some light, but the rock wasn't glowing anymore. And it was completely cool to the touch, but not icy cold. Just like a normal rock that I might have picked up on the bank of the creek.

"Hm," Arun grunted, looking down at the stone in my hand. "That's weird."

Weird, but not bad. I chose to believe that it had stopped working because we'd finally arrived. "The heir has to be here. That's the only explanation."

Estrid was already moving forward, her hand on the hilt of her sword though she dared not draw it again. It was more of a security thing, I thought.

I pocketed the stone and followed her. The house was nothing special: a small living area with a hearth and a dining table on the eastern wall. There was one bedroom in the back, divided from the living area with a screen, and another in a loft accessible by a small wooden ladder, like where I'd slept with Erik and Estrid in our childhood home before Erik got too old to sleep with his sisters and started sleeping on a pallet by the hearth.

Arun was at the hearth. He touched the ashes. The tips of his fingers came away sooty and black. He peered in the pot hanging over the hearth. "Cold and empty," he said.

Estrid emerged from the back bedroom. "The bed is unmade. Seems like maybe there were three women living here based on the clothes in the wardrobes."

I climbed the ladder to the loft. There were two straw mattresses, both topped with fleece blankets. One bed was meticulously made. The other's blanket was thrown to one side, and the pillow still had the indent of a head that had been sleeping there. The rest of the room was littered with pieces of paper. Each paper held a sketch done in confident lines of black coal. There was the house and the creek and the grasslands. There were eyes and hands and full faces of old women with wrinkles around their mouths, and a younger girl with an easy smile. And there was one—only one—of another young girl, this one with big eyes and curly dark hair. I picked it up from the floor and studied it. The face looked strikingly like the one I'd seen staring back at me from the scrying pool. Then I looked at the mess all around me. Had she drawn these? Was this her easy life, hidden behind a protection spell?

Suddenly, I wanted to rip the drawings to shreds and burn the pieces in the hearth. She'd stolen that easy life from me, turned me into something I never wanted just so she could survive, so she could carry on Onen Suun's legacy.

I hated her.

But I had also promised to help her.

Leaving the drawings behind, I rejoined Estrid and Arun in the living area. "She's not here."

"No," Arun agreed, "but she was."

"Now what?"

Estrid smiled. "Now, we track her."

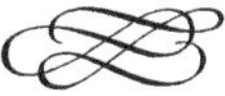

CHAPTER 17

I was only three when I realized I would never win a game of hide-and-seek when I was playing with Estrid. Only a few years older than I, she could already track anything as well as the hunting dogs some of the D'ahvol kept. Our father had never had a wounded deer or boar escape, because Estrid would always find it, through rain, snow, or darkness. That was why, when she knelt outside the cabin and pressed her fingers to an impression there that I hadn't even noticed, I knew we would find the heir in spite of the fact the sun was already heading down for the day.

She looked up and squinted, as if that helped her see farther. "They went west."

Away from the way we'd come, into new territory, then.

"How many?" I asked.

Estrid took a few steps forward, keeping low to the ground. She passed through the gate and turned left, studying a place where the grass had been stamped down. "Four. Four women. Running."

"Wait." Only four? If there'd been three downstairs and two in the loft, we were missing one.

My sister, who had been ready to follow the trail, looked up at me. "What?"

I remembered what else we'd seen in the scrying pool, the old woman's dead body. I cut through the garden, trying and failing not to stomp on any of the plants. The first thing I saw when I rounded the back of the house was the mound of freshly disturbed dirt. A grave. I was silent as I stared across the yard at it, remembering the priest's dull, grey eyes. How did she die? If I'd gotten here sooner, would she still be alive? It seemed to be screaming at me, *too late, too late, too late!*

Estrid pulled me back. "We need to hurry, find the others before they meet the same fate. The tracks are already a few days old."

Arun and I fell in behind Estrid. He leaned over and asked, "How does she know?"

I shrugged. "It's all to do with the depth of the print, the direction of the grass, things like that. Most people just see them on the surface for what they are, but she sees stories in them."

When we entered a copse of the flat-topped trees, Estrid ran her fingers across the bark and then picked a scrap of linen from a nearby thorn poking out of the underbrush. Orange, like the robes of the priests.

"Let's keep going," I urged.

Eventually, we reached an open field where their path was obvious, so we ran, following the trail of trampled grasses. We turned south at a narrow river and crossed at a wooden bridge. Someone had dropped a purple flower halfway across the bridge, and I remembered seeing this same plant in the yard. It seemed like something the artist might do—stop to pluck a flower before running for her life. I kicked it off into the water, where it quickly sank out of view.

Estrid picked up the trail again on the other side, moving slower now that the world had sunk into twilight. We were getting farther and farther from the cabin, and I wondered just how far the protective bubble extended. If these women had lived inside it for the last couple of decades, they were not ready to face what lay waiting for them in the outside world. They likely had no way of knowing they were running straight into danger.

Eventually, we happened upon another copse of trees, this one beside a wider, cleaner river. On the riverbank was a circle of rocks and, though the ashes had been scattered, what was clearly the remains of a campfire. Estrid examined the ashes and the tracks around the campsite.

"We're gaining ground on them," she declared. "This must have been last night's campsite."

Arun collapsed on a nearby log. "Still a day away at least, though."

"At least," Estrid agreed. Then, she looked at me. "Do you want to stop or keep going and try to catch them by morning?"

I wanted to keep going, but Estrid and Arun looked as exhausted as I felt. "We can stop," I said. "Why don't we make camp here and leave before dawn to try to gain on them some more?"

While Estrid worked on the fire, Arun went with me to the river to see if we could catch anything for dinner.

"Are you and your sister okay?" He asked when we stopped on the riverbank to take off our boots and roll up our pants.

"Yes." I hadn't said anything earlier because I was worried that talking about it might lead to a conversation about *us*, and I was not ready for that.

"And she's okay with," he waved his hand back and forth between us. "With this?"

I cringed. "Hmm, 'okay' might be a strong word."

He laughed. "'Okay' is probably the most generic word I could have used."

"She'll be fine with it. Just give her time."

We waded into the water until it came up to below our

knees. It was cold, but bearable. I stooped low, letting my fingers dangle in the water. He did the same beside me.

"Have you ever caught a fish like this?" he asked.

I hushed him. "You can't talk. The vibrations will scare the fish away."

A few more moments passed, and then, in a whisper, he asked, "Well, have you?"

I tried not to smile but couldn't help it. "Yes."

He made an impressed grunt.

"How do elves catch fish?" I whispered. "Do you just *magic* them into your hands?"

"Is magic a verb now?"

"I don't know what magic is." And I didn't know what Arun's magic was, in spite of elves typically being very magical creatures.

Something brushed my fingers and I grew still and quiet. Arun seemed to sense it because he did, too. We studied the dark water, waiting for a flash of movement. It was Arun who moved suddenly, hands grasping, and then he pulled a fish from the water, grasping it between two hands. He smiled over at me.

I laughed. "You magicked it, didn't you?"

"I'll never tell."

Estrid had the fire burning hotly by the time we got back. Arun cleaned the fish, and I found sticks we could use to roast the meat. We sat in companionable silence, cooking strips of fish over the flames. When we were done, I volunteered to carry the skin and bones away from the camp so that any animals that liked the smell of them would be drawn away from us.

It was a short walk through the woods back to the river. I walked upriver for a few minutes before digging a hole and burying the fish remains. The night was eerily still and quiet here in the boundaries of the protection spell. Not even birds were singing in the trees. Every now and then, a breeze rustled the grasses, sounding too much like someone stalking me.

I was hurrying on my way back, which was why I tripped over something heavy that sent me sprawling in the dirt. As soon as my boot connected with whatever it was, even as I was falling, my mind supplied the word "body." There was no mistaking the soft, fleshy feel. My first reaction was to draw my ax, but a shocking jolt sent it flying from my hand. After that, I couldn't stop convulsing. It was like the protection spell had decided I was a threat, even without the ax. I must have made some noise because Arun appeared, followed by Estrid, both of them dropping to their knees beside me just as the sensation subsided and I curled into a ball on the ground. Tears were involuntarily running down my cheeks.

Arun wiped them away with his thumbs. "What happened?"

"B-b-body," I stammered.

Estrid rose slowly to her feet and scanned the riverbank. I knew the moment she found it, when she froze and even her breathing got quieter.

I was catching my breath and my heart rate was slowing.

Arun propped me up against him and brushed hair back from my face.

"Who is it?" I asked. I could see its shape now, someone sprawled face down in the mud.

Estrid moved finally, going to kneel beside the body. "Another priest," she answered. "A woman in orange robes."

I closed my eyes. Two of the women charged with protecting the heir were dead. It was obvious we were on the right trail, but the odds were not looking good. What if the stone hadn't stopped working because we'd arrived, but because the person it was meant to find had died?

No. I wouldn't let myself think that. "Help me up," I demanded.

Arun grabbed me under the arms and pulled me up with him. My legs were still shaky under me, but he kept his arm around me, looping one of my arms around his neck. Had it been anyone else, I would have protested, but not Arun. I would let Arun take care of me. I even let him pick up my ax and stick it back in my belt. For whatever reason, the protection spell didn't zap him.

Back at camp, Estrid extinguished the campfire. "We should have been safe here, but it looks like something got past the protection spell."

"Bruhier is a tricky place," I said, because we could all use a reminder. "Could you see how she died?" It wasn't pleasant to think about, but it would help if we knew what we were up against.

She shook her head. "Not really. Too much blood."

I moaned. "Great."

Arun still hadn't let go of me. His face looked drawn in the blue light of Gleet, which was huge on the southern horizon.

"I know you guys wanted to rest, but I don't think we can. We need to go, and we need to hurry. I want to try to get to the heir before whatever is picking them off gets to her, too."

Neither of them argued and we set off behind Estrid. This time, I vowed, I would pay attention to what was in front of me.

We walked through the night. It was slow going but we didn't take any breaks except for when we had to pause for Estrid to pick up the trail again. It seemed to keep to the river, veering every now and then into the grasses but always coming back to the water. When the sun had risen and we'd stopped to fill our canteens in the river, I found another purple flower, this one barely visible in the mud. I would have missed it except that it stuck to the sole of my boot and floated to the top of the water when I stepped close to the river. It drifted away before I could catch it. I didn't say anything to the others.

That was what they felt like: "others." Even though we were on the same side, even though we had the same goal, and even though I loved them both, the closer we got to discovering the fate of the heir, the more I felt like I wasn't one of them. They could walk away at any time. But not me. I was connected to the heir, and if she wa dead, it would be up to me to figure out what would come next. I was the one with the target on my face. But until I knew otherwise, I had to believe she was alive, and I had to believe that together, she and I would be able to do something about the evil that was coming. Estrid wanted to protect me, but everything I did was to protect her and everyone I loved.

While I was still filling my canteen, Estrid wandered away, following the trail that turned into the grasses. When she was gone, Arun waded over to where I was and took the canteen from my hands, tossing it with his on the riverbank.

"What are you doing?" I asked.

He didn't answer. Instead, he took my face in his hands and kissed me. His hands slid down my neck to my shoulders, then my waist, where they pulled me flush against him. I went from stunned and resistant to putty in his hands. The water rushed around our ankles as if we were a part of the landscape, just two immovable boulders.

Finally, I pulled away with a gasp. "What was that for?"

"When I saw you on the ground beside that body, I thought… That could be you. It could be me. It could be any of us. So, I wanted to kiss you while I still could. So that if something happens to me, you'll have no doubt."

"Nothing is going to happen to you."

He laughed.

I smacked his arm and pushed him away. "Nothing is going to happen to you. Or to anyone. I won't let it."

Grabbing for me, he pulled me back against him. "I believe you," he said against my mouth just before he kissed me again.

"Frida!" Estrid's shout sliced through the quiet morning air like a punch to the gut.

I broke free from Arun and ran to the riverbank. He was right behind me but stopped to pick up the canteens and fell behind. I followed Estrid's trail through the grasses. It didn't take me long to realize I was actually following the trail of something much larger.

Estrid stood on the edge of a huge clearing of stamped down grass and mud. I pulled up right behind her, putting my hands on her shoulders to stop myself. Across from us was the prone body of a manticore, its belly ripped open and its guts spilling out. Just a few feet from it was another body, this one with the familiar blue skin of an ur'gel. Though it was humanoid in shape and appearance, it was about twice as large as me, with huge, muscled arms, and black wings poking out of its shoulders. The wings were sliced to ribbons, and there were five huge gashes across its chest and stomach.

"Looks like they did each other in," I said.

"Was it just the two of them?" Arun asked.

"I didn't—"

But Estrid didn't get to finish. Before she could, another manticore burst out of the grasses beside us and roared, a rumbling bellow that shook the ground. One of its wings was broken and dragged along the ground. I stumbled back, pulling Estrid with me just as it raked its claws in our direction. It missed, and I noticed that its face was bloody, its eyes closed. The ur'gel had likely blinded it before it died, leaving us to deal with one angry manticore.

"It can't see," I whispered. "Move."

We scrambled backward and ran, splitting up and taking three different directions through the grasses. I turned to see which way it went and was glad to see that it followed me. I couldn't draw my ax, but I could run and climb and swim. I would get away, or I would die trying. At least I would save Estrid and Arun.

For a blind manticore, it was fast, though of course it had the advantage of four legs. Since it couldn't see, I zigzagged in an attempt to confuse it, which only served to make it angrier. I finally reached the river and splashed into it, kicking up my feet and propelling myself into the middle, where the current picked me up and carried me downriver a bit. The manticore was undeterred. He plunged in after me and gained on me quickly, turning out to be a powerful swimmer.

The current sped up and it was nearly on top of me. I was trying to decide what to do when another scream split the air, this one familiar and welcome. Stiarna was diving toward us, claws outstretched, and wings tucked in tight. She landed on the manticore and both of them went under for a few moments before bobbing to the surface in a flurry of teeth and claws. I pushed away from them as best as I could, but it wasn't easy. The current was strong enough to pull me under.

I bobbed back to the surface. "Stiarna!" I shouted.

The two of them were rolling and splashing. When Stiarna got her wings out from under the manticore, it used its massive jaws to drag her back under. The water around them swirled red with blood. I did my best to stay afloat, to keep my eyes on them, but it was getting harder and I was getting tired. Above the splashing and the snarling, I heard a loud, crashing sound, and I knew what it was.

"Stiarna," I said again, quieter this time, less hopeful. We were coming up on a waterfall.

The griffin searched for me, called to me, and was then dragged back under.

I managed to grab a tree branch that was hanging over the water and dragged myself up onto it. I shielded my eyes with my hands and found the drop-off, saw where the river disappeared into the mist and plunged down the cliff, but I didn't see Stiarna or the manticore. I shimmied to the tree trunk and down onto the riverbank, then ran the few dozen yards to where the water fell.

There was no sign of them.

Stiarna was gone.

She'd saved me so many times, and I had done nothing to keep her safe. I'd just told Arun that I wouldn't let anything happen to anyone, and yet here I was. Tears pricked my eyes and I swiped at them angrily. Arun and Estrid appeared beside me.

"Was that Stiarna?" Arun asked, peering down the cliff.

I nodded, not trusting my voice. Below us, nothing moved except for the foaming water flowing away from us.

He put a hand on my back. "I'm sorry."

"Me, too," Estrid added. "But where did she come from?"

I pointed to the sky.

Arun nodded as if that made sense. "The protection spell set boundaries on the ground, not in the air. No one expected ur'gels, I guess."

Who would? Who would expect any of this?

"We're close to the edge," Arun continued. "Of the spell. I can feel the charge."

He was right. We followed Estrid back to where the ur'gel and the manticore lay, then picked up the trail to continue west. Soon, we passed the barrier, a surge of energy pulsing around us. To test it, Estrid drew her sword. Nothing happened.

I drew my own ax but felt no joy in it. I would just have to keep on killing, and Stiarna would keep on being dead, and Erik would keep on being gone, and I couldn't protect anyone.

Arun's hand on my shoulder brought me back and he pulled me into a hug while Estrid searched for the trail.

"I am so sorry," he said again.

"She was just an animal," I said into his chest and immediately felt ashamed of myself.

He seemed to know. "She was a friend."

"Yes, she was." I was horrified to find myself sobbing, but I couldn't help it. My shoulders shook and he wrapped me into a hug. I was glad. At least that way, maybe Estrid wouldn't see it.

A few minutes later, after I had somewhat composed myself, she reappeared. "We have a problem."

"What now?" I asked with a groan. I knew my eyes were red and gross, but she didn't make any comment on it.

"There are two paths. One leads away, and the other leads back the way we came, toward the house."

I shook my head. "We can't split up."

"Try the stone. Maybe it will work again."

I didn't think so, but I wasn't about to argue. I pulled it and the compass out of my shirt and held them together. The compass worked fine. The stone was dead.

Estrid took the stone and tossed it aside. It landed in the dirt with a thump. "We have to split up."

She was right. We had no way of knowing which way the heir went. Maybe her guardians had walked her to the boundary and turned her lose on the world. Or maybe they'd split up, too, to throw the ur'gels off their track, and she went back to the house.

"I'll go that way." Estrid pointed west, away from the house. "Frida, you go back to the house. Arun—"

"I'm with Frida," he said, leaving no room for debate.

Before Estrid could turn away, I grasped her forearm. She looked down at it, surprised, before grasping mine. "Be safe," I said to her.

She smiled. "Be brave."

We let go of each other and she stalked away. I watched her until she was a speck on the horizon, and then turned to follow my own path.

CHAPTER 19

"The world is full of stories," Estrid had said when she'd been trying to teach me to track in the jungle below Barepost. "You just have to be able to see them."

I was looking for that story now, trying to put myself in the heir's shoes, to understand where she'd gone and why. Why had she doubled back, what had happened to her and her guardians? Part of me was afraid to find the answer.

"There." I pointed to a half-circle in the mud, the imprint of a toe. The heel had barely touched the ground. She was running. "And there." The small crescents were fairly easy to follow once I knew what to look for. They cut a straight line across the field, disappearing into some trees. We followed a path of trampled leaves and in one place, a curly black hair snagged on a tree branch. I kept my eyes open for more of the purple flowers, but there were none.

I was useless after night fell and was afraid to lose the trail, so we camped by the riverbank. We couldn't light a fire for fear of attracting a flying predator, so we ate some berries Arun had gathered and sat huddled side-by-side for warmth. He took first watch, so I slept with my head on his shoulder. He woke me when Aupra was directly overhead, and then curled around me to sleep.

Here, in the open field, the darkness was almost a tangible thing, another creature. More than once I was tempted to shout a *hello* into the night just to see if anyone answered. I didn't for fear of what might. Part of me expected Stiarna to tumble out of the grasses and glare at me while she licked blood off her feathers. But another part of me knew she was gone. The manticore had been twice her size. She hadn't stood a chance against it, but she'd still thrown herself fearlessly into the fight. It made me think of my own mother, who had died trying to protect me, and I wondered if maybe a part of her had lived on in the griffin.

Overhead, the stars winked at me. I occupied myself by counting them and tracing shapes between them until they disappeared with the dawn.

I woke Arun and we continued on our search. Once, we crossed our own path from the day before when we'd been headed in the opposite direction. I wondered if the heir had enough training to spot our tracks. If she did, though, it hadn't changed her trajectory. If she was going back to the house, we might even reach her before she arrived.

The sun had completely risen in front of us, an orange ball glowing on the horizon, when a growl ripped through the air. Without hesitating, Arun and I launched ourselves forward, racing through the grasses toward the sound, no longer careful to follow the tracks.

The first thing we saw was a gutspider, with its long, stick-like legs and fat, grotesque body. Below it, facing its gaping jaws, was a woman. Her shrill scream drew us forward even quicker.

"We can't draw our weapons," I said to Arun, still running.

"Maybe...," he paused, gasping for air. "Maybe if we're protecting the heir." To test it, he drew his bow and an arrow.

Nothing happened to him, even as he nocked the arrow and let it fly into the creature's backside.

The gutspider screamed and stumbled, its long, spindly legs flailing. Another of Arun's arrows pierced its belly and it toppled sideways. The girl beneath it scrambled to her feet, and…

Laughed?

Savarah.

That bitch.

She stood, brushing off her light pink dress and smoothing down her golden curls. And emerging out of the grass behind her, a winged ur'gel. That was how she got in here. Her other one must have been killed by the manticore.

We stopped several yards away.

"That was close," she called to us. "Thank you, elf. I suppose I'm glad I didn't kill you earlier after all. Though I'll have to pay Ravyn a visit and learn how she beat the dark magic. I was sure you would have been one of mine by now."

"Light will always defeat dark," I growled at her, hating the idea of Arun being one of her brainless minions, and hating even more how close he'd come.

Hate. Anger. Resentment. They boiled up inside of me. I reached inside the collar of my shirt and pulled out the locket. As soon as it was visible, I felt my heart rate slow, felt my reasoning return. It apparently didn't even have to be open to work.

Savarah scowled at it.

"What now?" Arun asked. He'd put away his bow and arrow and drew his sword.

I pulled my own sword and ax from my belt. "She's mine. You take the ur'gel."

"Gladly."

The ur'gel met Arun head on, while Savarah was not so eager to engage in hand-to-hand combat. She kept a few paces away from me and never turned her back on me. I could feel her trying to get a read on me and manipulate my feelings, but her powers bounced off me, thanks to the locket. I was going to kill her, and I was going to be in my right mind when I did it.

She decided to try another tactic. "I've killed the priests you sought, the ones who could help you with your abilities. You'll never learn how to seal the prison as Onen Suun did."

I held in a sigh of relief. She hadn't figured it out. She still thought I was the heir. That meant she didn't know that one of the women in the cabin had been the heir. But if she'd killed them all, then that meant that the heir was among those numbers, unless the girl had escaped.

"Here, let me show you the last one."

Savarah stepped to the side and revealed the form of a young woman in traveling clothes, not the orange robes of a priest. She had black hair, and her dark eyes stared back at me lifelessly. Her throat was ripped open, her hands stained red with her own blood.

It was her. It had to be. How could I deny it any longer? All of this had been for nothing. Stiarna had died … for nothing. Dag'draath would keep hunting me until I was dead, and there was no one alive who could stop him. Not even me.

For a crazy second, I considered putting the locket away and letting the rage take over and carry me away. I just wanted her dead. If I could just take her with me, then maybe it would all be okay.

The ur'gel that Arun was fighting gave a howl that drew our attention to their fight. Arun's sword was through its chest and protruding out its back, the tip gleaming black with ur'gel blood. Arun used his foot to kick the monster off. It fell to its back, dead.

But Savarah, who'd just lost her ride out of here, wasn't upset. In fact, she was smiling at something over my head. I turned and saw another ur'gel in the sky, bearing down on us. I ducked as it passed overhead and scooped up Savarah, carrying her into the sky and out of my reach.

Savarah gave me a small finger wave. "I'm not going to kill you, Frida Svand, not yet. First, I will destroy all those you love and cherish." Her laugh sent chills down my spine.

"Shoot her," I demanded.

Arun shook his head. "She's too far already."

"Shoot her!" I jerked the bow out of his hands and nocked an arrow that I leveled at the distant dot that was Savarah and her ur'gel. He was right. To make it worse my hands were shaking so badly I wouldn't have been able to hit her if she were standing two feet in front of me.

It was the threat that had done it. I'd let her get away, and now she was going to kill someone—everyone—I loved. My father, Erik, Estrid, Xalph, Grissall. Anyone I'd ever had the nerve to feel any love for, they were all in danger, and I was stuck here in the grasslands with nothing but the body of the Suun heir and the remains of any hope I'd had bleeding out on the ground.

CHAPTER 20

I dropped to my knees beside the woman on the ground and fruitlessly check for a pulse.

Nothing.

The ur'gel had all but ripped her throat out, and Savarah hadn't even known the truth of who she was. The only good that came out of her death, I supposed, was that now she couldn't be used against the Light to free Dag'draath.

Assuming she was the heir.

She certainly didn't look like a priest. No orange robe or golden bangles. She was just a regular girl. I touched her temple, where the mark had once been. It was cold and bare. This had to be why the rock stopped working. Because she was dead. There was no point to this mission anymore. Everything I'd done to get us here had been for nothing.

Arun didn't say anything or offer any comfort, which was fine by me. I didn't want any pity. Instead, we gathered dead grasses and after making a decent pile, laid the body on top of the straw. Then we went to a nearby copse of trees and collected branches, which we placed around the body. Even though the heir wasn't D'ahvol, she would receive a proper

Ahvoli funeral pyre. It was easier than burying the body, which I thought the priests did. It didn't make sense to me, though. If they worshiped the light, why did they want to rest for eternity in the dark? It was better this way, and there was no one to argue with me.

Arun lit the straw with a flint rock and his knife. It caught and spread quickly over the dry grass. We'd made sure to dampen the area around the body so the fire wouldn't spread. It worked, keeping the flames contained to the straw and sticks, and eventually, the body.

We stood back and watched. I covered my mouth and nose with a handkerchief and beside me, Arun did the same.

"Do you want to say anything?" he asked, raising his eyebrows over his handkerchief.

"Like what?"

He shrugged. "I don't know. It's just … it just feels like there should be …"

"Something else?" I offered. I knew what he meant, even if I wasn't being exceedingly kind about it. This was what our mission had been reduced to. A dead girl and a funeral pyre. Not just a dead girl, I corrected myself. A dead *Suun*.

Seeing I wasn't going to say anything, Arun stepped closer to her. "I hope. I hope you are reunited with your family. With Onen Suun. Let the light guide you home."

When he stepped back beside me, I leaned my head on his shoulder, feeling deflated. "That was nice."

He smiled at me, but it was a sad smile.

We left soon after that, leaving the column of black smoke snaking away into the sky. I wondered if it would even be able to reach past the veil, and if it did, what Quynn would think. If Quynn was even still hanging around. We'd been down here a long time. I wouldn't fault her for leaving. It wasn't exactly a fruitful adventure.

When night fell again, we made camp by the river. I felt

disgusting, coated in sweat and ur'gel blood. I smelled like ashes and burned flesh, and Arun wasn't much better.

"Come on," I told him, leading him to the muddy riverbank. I unbuckled my weapons belts and laid them on a rock, then took off my leather jerkin and folded it on top of them.

"What are you doing?" Arun asked.

"Taking a bath." I stripped until all I was wearing was the ublarite necklace. I had never been modest or ashamed of my body. The D'ahvol saw a body as a vessel, as a weapon, as something to use to enjoy the pleasures of this world before passing onto the next and leaving it behind. But standing in front of Arun, who was still fully clothed, bathed in Gleet's blue moonlight, I had the sudden urge to cover myself.

His eyes wandered over every curve, every muscle, every scar—and there were a lot of them. All of them earned.

"Are you coming?" I asked, forcing myself to turn away and wade into the cool water.

I heard him unbuckling but didn't turn around until I was already submerged to my shoulders. He was wading in by then, the water reaching his waist. His chiseled chest was bare, and his hair was loose around his face. He ducked beneath the water and emerged brushing it back, dripping wet. I shivered, and it wasn't because I was cold.

When he reached me, his arms came around me and his lips met mine almost simultaneously. I ran my fingers through his wet hair and fisted it at the back of his neck. His hands pressed against my lower back and I lifted my legs, wrapping them around his waist. There was no space between us. It was impossible to tell where one of us began and the other ended.

I wanted to give myself to someone else and he was glad to take me just as I was, to take some of the burden and put it on his own shoulders. His hands stroked my back, my sides, my legs, and wherever he touched, my skin burned for him. I didn't feel cold or lonely or sad. I was hungry.

Fierce.

Careless.

He pulled away, breathless. "Are you sure?"

I opened my eyes. His were wide and dark, staring back at me. As hungry as I was. "Yes."

It was a long time before we emerged from the water, our fingers as wrinkled as prunes. I no longer felt compelled to cover myself and collapsed naked on the dry grass. The veil was thin, and I could make out the stars beyond them.

"I'll take first watch," Arun said, standing over me, his hair dripping, the water running in sparkling rivulets down his arms.

I reached up and pulled him down with me. "Just sleep with me."

"But…"

"I want to be with you." I wanted to sleep as well as I had on the ship, tucked beneath his arm. I didn't want to dream about ur'gels and dead girls and worst of all, Savarah and her promises.

He gave in, and when I woke in the morning, I couldn't remember dreaming. We dressed in silence, but we didn't turn away from each other or try to hide. As we walked, following the path to where we'd left Estrid, we kept finding reasons to touch each other, whether it was to get my attention or to pull him forward to look at something I'd found. Eventually, I simply slipped my hand into his, twining our fingers together, and walked beside him.

We passed the place where we'd left Estrid and followed her trail to the west. She'd left an easy trail on purpose, squishing plants and turning over rocks, so that we would be able to find her if we beat her back. Even as the world sank into twilight, I was able to keep the trail. I had to look closer, though, and that was how I saw it, the purple petal on the side of the trail.

"Oh, no," I muttered under my breath, bending to touch it. I squeezed it beneath my fingers, my mind racing. It was the same as the others. Was it her? Had we been wrong?

"What is it?" Arun glanced over my shoulder. "A flower?"

"A purple flower. I found these earlier. By the house. On the trail. I thought maybe it was the heir dropping them."

He squinted down the trail into the growing dark. "That would mean..."

I nodded. I hated to feel glad that someone had died, but I was glad. Glad that maybe it hadn't been the heir, after all. I didn't know why there would have been another girl in plain clothes with the priests. Unless ...

Unless she'd been a decoy.

"I could be wrong," I hastened to say.

"Or you could be right."

"I could be right."

We went quicker after that. If the heir was out here, I was sure Estrid had found her. But where were they now?

At a curve in the trail, we came across something blocking our path. At first, it seemed to be a rock. But as we neared, I noticed the row of spikes across the top.

"What is that?" Arun asked, putting his hand on it.

"A blazetaur," I told him. I didn't know why a blazetaur would be out here, in the middle of a field. They typically laid their eggs in places like this, but only when there were trees nearby that would hide their massive, armored bodies. I thought it was dead, not just sleeping, but to be safe, I followed the line of its back to the tail. The venomous stinger had been severed but was nowhere to be found. Had Estrid done this? I had no doubt she could fight and defeat a blazetaur single-handedly.

But then I looked past the tail, to the other side of the blaze-taur. It was another body. I stepped over the tail, careful not to touch any of the venom leaking from the tip and hurried to the body.

An ur'gel, its throat slit.

And a few yards away, another ur'gel.

"Frida." Arun's voice was strained and high-pitched.

I didn't hesitate. I ran to where he stood farther down the path.

Before I could see what he was looking at, he turned and grabbed me by the shoulders. "No."

"What?" Bile rose in my throat. "What is it?"

"No," he repeated.

But I could see it on his face.

His hands tightened on my arms as I struggled, until finally he scooped me up in a hug. "I'm sorry. I'm sorry," he whispered into my ear repeatedly, but I couldn't hear him anymore.

Over his shoulder, I saw her. Estrid, lying on her back in the dirt. She wasn't moving. Her chest wasn't rising and falling with breath. Her eyes didn't flutter with sleep.

With a shove, I freed myself from Arun and dropped to Estrid's side.

"Estrid," I gasped, shaking her. "Estrid."

My hands searched her body and found three long gashes in her stomach and another one in her leg. The ground around her was soaked and warm with spilled blood.

Arun squatted behind me, not speaking, and not touching me.

"No," I muttered, rocking back on my heels. "No, no, no, no." This wasn't happening. I tried to catch my breath but found it nearly impossible.

Be safe.

Be brave.

Be *alive*.

I never knew I had to say that. I never even knew she could be gone.

But here was her body, lifeless and unmoving. Proof that sometimes the unbelievable became the reality.

I would never hear her voice again. She would never see

Bor'sur or Father or Erik again. She would never be an aunt or a mother or a wife. She would never challenge me or push me again.

And why was I spared? I was nothing. A fraud. A fake. A false heir. A failure as a sister. I couldn't protect anyone.

She still held a sword in one hand, and I lifted her arm, crossing it over her chest. I lifted her other hand and brought it up, too, only to find her fingers wrapped around something. A piece of cloth. I pried her fingers open and pulled the cloth out, holding it close to examine it in the dark.

It was light pink.

I remembered Savarah's pale hands running over her skirts, dusting off her dress the same color as this cloth.

The wail bubbled up inside of me and burst forth, louder and more primal than any animal's call. Arun tried to wrap his arms around my shoulders, but I shoved him off, pushing to my feet and stumbling away.

"Savarah!" I shouted into the sky. "Savarah!" I shouted until my throat was raw and her name came out as a hoarse, raspy whisper. I wanted her to come. I wanted her to face me, and I wanted to kill her. I didn't care how powerful she was or how many hundreds of years she'd lived, she would die for this, and I would be the one to do it. I would be the one to drain the life from her eyes. I would put an end to her reign of terror. I didn't care about Dag'draath. Savarah was the real villain. Her life was mine.

This revenge was mine. This anger, this fury, this hatred.

And this sorrow.

I tucked them all inside of me and collapsed beside my sister, my head on her chest as I cried and begged her to come back.

CHAPTER 21

It was morning when Arun pulled me away from Estrid's body, cooing gentle words I refused to hear.

In spite of everything, I had not turned to him for comfort last night. After he'd endured all he could of the silent treatment, he'd left me to my sorrow and spent the night building a proper funeral pyre, one that reached as high as some of the nearby trees. And at the bottom, beneath the tower of branches, he'd left just enough space for a body.

For my *sister's* body.

The thought sent me back into hysterics and I tried to throw myself down on Estrid, but Arun had a firm grip on me.

"Let go!" I howled at him, beating my fists against his chest. "Let go of me! I hate you! If I hadn't been with you, I could have helped her. She died alone and I hate you."

It wasn't true. I hated only myself.

The words stung him even though he tried to hide it. It made me hate myself even more.

But I couldn't stop. "This is what will happen. To everyone who loves me." Savarah's threat was fresh in my mind, her cruel laugh the only sound I could hear over the blood rushing in my ears.

"No, it won't," Arun objected.

"I'm a poison." I tugged but he still held my wrists tight against his chest. "I'm death."

"That's not true." His brow was furrowed and there were dark circles of sleeplessness under his eyes.

I took a deep, gasping breath and doubled over, knocking my head against his chest.

He let go of my wrists, only to wrap me up in a tight hug. My shoulders shook with sobs, but he didn't let go, like he could squeeze the pain away. It halfway worked. The tightness in my chest subsided and my breathing became more regular, even if it was still shaky. Finally, I wrapped my arms around his waist and took a deep breath.

"It's not your fault," Arun said, his voice gentle and cautious. "None of this is your fault."

I wanted to believe him, but Estrid's body was evidence to the contrary.

We didn't have anything to use as a shroud, but I found two small stones to cover her eyes and made sure her sword was in her hands and crossed over her chest so that it would go with her to the next life. I braided her hair the way that she liked it and washed the ur'gel blood from her hands and face. Arun tried to help me carry her to the pyre, but I pushed him away, taking her in my arms and carrying her there myself. Laying her gently on the straw and arranging her just so amidst the branches.

Arun handed me his flint, but I sat there for a long time with it in my hands, staring down at my sister. Her body had gotten colder and stiffer. She wasn't in there anymore, but it was still hard to let go.

Finally, I struck the flint against my ax and blew on the sparks that landed in the dry grass beneath her. They caught and began to spread. I stepped back and watched the flames dance, layer after layer of the pyre catching until the heat was so intense, I had to move away even farther, back to where Arun stood. He looked at me sideways, expecting me to burst into tears, but the time for that had passed. I wouldn't waste any more energy on tears and sadness. Everything had to go toward getting revenge on Savarah.

The Suun heir was dead, Estrid was dead, Stiarna was dead. And Erik? Erik was gone, maybe dead if Savarah had gotten to him. The wayfinder's stone was of no more use to us. We would call Quynn down and report our failure, and then what? I couldn't go home, but I also couldn't stay on the *Wind Wraith* and risk everyone's lives. Quynn probably wouldn't let me, besides. I couldn't go back to Barepost and lead Savarah there, where she would discover the production of the ublarite trinkets. I couldn't go to Lunla or Ravyn and risk bringing Savarah's wrath down on the temples, either. What I had to do was find somewhere new, somewhere empty, where Savarah and I could play out our final battle eventually.

The pyre smoldered all day, and I watched the smoke disappear into the veil, only moving to sit down when my legs wouldn't hold me any longer. Arun busied himself with catching and cooking a couple of fish that he offered to me. I ate them, but they sat like rocks in my empty, roiling stomach.

"Do you have the horn?" Arun asked eventually, when we were just a few hours from sunset.

I did. It had been hanging from Estrid's belt. I handed it to him.

"Let's head back to the spot where she dropped us off and see if she's still around to hear us."

"Fine." The sooner I could get up there, the sooner I could get Arun to safety and get myself away from everyone to ensure their safety. "Let me go wash up."

Arun didn't come this time.

I cut a straight path to where the river wound through a copse of trees, and dipped my hands into the cool water, splashing it on my swollen eyes. If I thought about Estrid too hard, I would start crying again, so I squeezed my eyes shut and told myself to lock her away. Not to forget about her, but to put her in a special place where I would keep the memory of her, but not mourn her constantly.

A noise to my left startled me. I wiped hastily at my face and turned to look, seeing nothing.

"Arun?" I asked the low brush around me.

No one responded.

I stood and the noise came again. It almost sounded like a hiccup, like the remnants of tears. I was familiar with that sound today. I took a few steps along the river, and then paused to listen again. There, barely audible over the sound of the water but very close. To my right was a sharp drop-off where the river had carved away at the surrounding land. I took a step down, turned, and locked eyes with her where she was pressed against the dirt, tucked beneath a fat root that made a sort of overhang.

Wide eyes, gentle features, curly hair decorated with purple flowers.

It was the girl from the scrying pool.

I blinked, shocked. "Hi."

She screamed, kicked out with one foot, and sent me sprawling backward into the river.

CHAPTER 22

Water closed over my face and I sputtered, coughing, and pushed myself to a sitting position. My tailbone and the palms of my hands hurt where I'd landed on the rocks, and I was soaking wet. When I looked at her again, she let loose another scream loud enough to wake the dead. And certainly, loud enough to alert any lingering ur'gels to our presence.

"Shut up." I lunged at her, slow because of the water drenching my clothes, and tackled her, pressing a hand over her mouth.

Her eyes went wide and panicky, but she stopped screaming. Instead, she froze in my arms. In the mountains around Bor'sur, there were some farms that kept small goats that would pretend to be dead if they were startled. It had been a game amongst the children when I was growing up to see who could scare the most goats into submission. That was exactly what she reminded me of.

Arun burst onto the riverbank a few seconds later, panting, his sword in his hand, his eyes wide as he searched for my attacker. He found us, and after deciding the goat girl posed no threat, tucked his sword away and waded through the water until he reached us.

He bent to look at us under the small overhang. "What's this?"

"Will you stop screaming?" I asked her.

She made no move and didn't acknowledge that she'd even heard me.

I slowly moved my hand away, but when I did, she took a big, gasping gulp, preparing herself for another outburst, so I clamped my hand back down.

"What is this?" Arun repeated.

"I don't know. I found her here. When she saw me, she started screaming."

"Why are you wet?"

I sighed. "Because she pushed me into the river."

Arun looked both amused and impressed.

I rolled my eyes. "I can't get anything out of her except a scream."

He knelt beside us, the mud squelching under his boots. "We won't hurt you. We want to help you. We're," he paused, taking in the rest of her. "Friends of the light."

I hadn't even noticed her clothes before that moment, but beneath the mud and the grime was an orange and white gown of a priest of light. At the words, she went limp in my hands and her breathing calmed. I hesitantly removed my hand, and when she didn't scream, I pushed myself off her, standing and reaching a hand down to her.

She took it. Her hand was small and her grip dainty as she pulled herself up to her feet. She barely came up to my shoulders.

Arun put a hand to his own chest. "I'm Arun." Gesturing to me, he added, "This is Frida."

The girl looked between us, then, in a shaky, breathy voice, said, "I'm Kaem. Kaem Naern."

Kaem Naern. I studied her, and she studied the ground. She was small, but not, I thought, as young as her small size made her seem. She had to be close to my age, but she was a priest, not the heir. We'd seen the heir's body, watched it burn.

Hadn't we? It seemed that she would be the only one with any answers.

"What are you doing here?" I asked her.

"I live here."

I flicked my eyes to the small hole where she'd been hiding. "Here?"

"In the cabin." She pointed vaguely to the east, golden bangles jangling on her wrists as she moved. "I've lived there my entire life with the priests."

"Are you a priest?" I asked.

She nodded. "My sisters and I serve the light."

"How many were you?"

"Five."

That meant she was the last one surviving. "And were there any among you who were not priests?"

She shrugged and shook her head. "There were three older women, Suze, Cladya, and Kensi, and then Daos and me. We were about the same age."

Arun reached out for her, but she flinched and shrank back, so he withdrew his hand. "Are you hungry? There's some food left at our camp if you want to sit and tell us your story. We'd like to know what happened, why you left the cabin, and how you came to be here, hiding by the river."

Kaem hesitated and then agreed with a small nod, not making eye contact with Arun. I realized that if she'd been here her entire life, then it was unlikely that she'd ever seen a man. Did Arun really look any different than the monsters she'd been running from?

I brought up the rear, and we followed Arun to the camp, where the funeral pyre was still burning. Kaem turned her eyes skyward, following the column of smoke, but didn't say anything or offer any condolences. I was glad. I didn't want to talk about it. Didn't want to tell her how Estrid had died for her, a priest. A nobody.

No, that wasn't true.

Estrid had died for me. Because I'd sent her after this girl. A fruitless errand.

Arun served the girl the remaining strips of fish and she ate them with gusto, licking her fingers and pulling bones from her teeth. I didn't know when she'd eaten last, but it seemed to have been an awfully long time. It wasn't until she was done that Arun sat down on one side of her and patted the space beside him, an invitation for me to join them. I did, dropping down onto the log and watching Kaem, who didn't make eye contact with either of us.

"Tell us," Arun started, "why did you leave the cabin?"

"The monsters came. Flying monsters, monsters that could get past the protection spell. Suze had told us about the monsters that lived on Bruhier, but we'd never thought to encounter them. We thought we were safe. Suze was out in the garden when they first came. She died casting a temporary protection spell around the house. Her sacrifice gave us a chance to escape."

The body in the garden, the woman we'd seen in the scrying pool.

"Where were you going to go?" Arun asked.

"I don't know exactly," Kaem said. "We were trying to reach one of the other temples on the island, run by priests they called Ravyn and Lunla."

"Have you ever met Ravyn or Lunla?" I asked.

She shook her head. "But they would be able to help us, they said."

"Then what happened? Why were you alone?"

"The monsters were hunting us. It was just three of us left."

She closed her eyes, and I knew she was seeing her friend's faces, reliving her last moments with them. "Cladya decided it would be best if we split up. She and Daos were going back to the cabin where they would reinforce the protection spells and hide. I was to go west until I reached a town, and then find passage to another temple and get help."

"From Lunla or Ravyn?"

"Right. From Lunla or Ravyn."

It sounded to me like Cladya and Daos had tried to act as distractions for the monsters, like they were trying to give Kaem a chance to get to safety. Why would they do that if she wasn't the heir? Had the other woman dressed in plain clothes been a decoy, or the real thing?

Arun leaned forward and rested his elbows on his knees, looking intently at Kaem even though she wouldn't look at us. "Were you and Daos treated the same? Did either of you get any … special attention?"

Kaem smiled. Even though her eyes were still wet with tears, the smile transformed her face from forlorn to dazzling. "Daos was better than me at everything. She was faster, stronger, smarter. So she got more in-depth training. I preferred to draw, read, and dream."

"What did you dream about?" I asked before Arun could speak up again.

"Freedom," she answered without missing a beat. "The world outside of our little bubble." She gestured at Arun. "Elves." Then, to me, "Warriors. Scholars. Lovers." Then, her smile drooped. "I never dreamt about this darkness, though."

No one did, I wanted to reassure her. No one ever imagined a darkness like this tainting their dreams. But especially not a girl who had grown up in such sheltered solitude.

Arun decided to get us back on track. "What happened here? With the monsters?"

I didn't know if I wanted to hear it, but I pressed my lips together and prepared myself anyway.

Kaem also didn't seem like she wanted to talk about it, but she spoke anyway, her words a low whisper. "She attacked from above."

"Who?"

"The beautiful woman with the golden hair. When she came, it felt … I felt different. I felt so desperate. So hopeless. I'd never been either of those things before."

Savarah, of course. I'd known, but it was nice to have confirmation.

"But then the other girl came, the one with the swords, the one who looks like you." She nodded at me and I felt my throat tighten. "She felled the giant spiked beast and then took on the others. I wanted to help, but I was a coward. She told me to run. So, I did. I watched her grab the golden-haired girl's dress, pull her back to her. She didn't see the winged man—"

"Ur'gel," Arun corrected her, probably not wanting any association with the monster.

"She didn't see the ur'gel until it was too late. He came up behind her and…"

I stood. "I get it. I get it. That's enough." It was. I didn't need a play-by-play of Estrid's death. She was more than a warrior to the rescue, than a body on the ground. "Did she escape? The golden-haired woman?"

"Yes. Yes, she escaped."

Good. It would have been nice if Estrid had finished her, but this way, revenge was still mine.

For the first time, Kaem looked sideways at Arun. "Now, can I ask a question, since I have answered yours?"

Arun nodded.

"Have you seen my sisters? Are they…?"

Arun's face must have told her what she needed to know, because she didn't finish her question.

"Excuse me," she muttered, as polite as ever. She stood and walked on silent feet to the crackling funeral pyre.

I followed, not wanting her to do something stupid.

But she stopped just short of the fire, where the heat was still bearable, and dropped to her knees. Her shoulders shuddered, and I realized she was crying. She'd grown up with those women. They'd been her mothers and her sisters, her best and only friends. It was strange to realize I knew how she felt, but that didn't mean I knew what to do for her. So, I stood vigil behind her, not touching her, not talking to her, but letting her grieve.

Watching her drop her face into her hands, I realized something else.

She was maybe the only person in the entire world who was more alone than I was.

CHAPTER 23

While Kaem grieved the loss of her sisters at my own sister's funeral pyre, Arun and I argued over what to do next.

"We can't use the horn," I said. "You'll bring the ur'gels down on our heads if the fire and her screaming haven't already alerted them."

"Quynn will get down here long before they can reach us. We have to get Kaem out of here." He grabbed my arm and pulled me closer to whisper in my ear, "She could be the heir."

Could be. Maybe. Possibly. None of those were good enough. "But she might not be."

"Are you willing to risk it? Let's just get her to Ravyn. She'll be able to tell us."

I chewed on my lip, my eyes on the girl's back. Was the fate of the world really on her narrow shoulders? "We need to get clear of here, and then find a way to higher ground before hailing Quynn."

Arun opened his mouth, probably to argue about wasting time and energy.

The girl's tiny, sing-song voice interrupted us. "What is that?" She was pointing into the sky.

I tilted my head back. Something wide and dark was breaking through the cloud cover, growing larger as it descended. My first thought was sky whale, but then the light hit it sideways and illuminated the wooden slats and the nets hanging from the hull.

"It's an airship," I told her.

She scurried over to where we were, ducking as if she might hit her head on the ship. "A what?"

"Like a trading ship, but it flies," Arun explained to her. He looked so triumphant I had the sudden urge to wipe the smug smile off his face with my fist.

Instead, I bit my lip and dug my fingernails into the palms of my hands. At least if the ur'gels came, we'd have backup.

The faces of sailors leaning over the railing came into view as the ship drew lower, some of them waving at us, some of them watching stoically, maybe assessing our newest member and realizing the identity of the one who was missing.

Quynn brought the ship down a safe distance away, and Arun and I made a run for it, Kaem trailing behind, her shorter legs slowing her down. The gangplank slid to the ground and Quynn disembarked first, Renwick at her side.

She looked us over coolly, her gaze pausing on Kaem. "Who is this?"

When I introduced them, Kaem gave a small curtsy and Quynn actually deigned to incline her head a fraction in acknowledgement.

"Where is Estrid?"

She's dead. The words lodged in my throat.

Arun saw me struggling. "She," but it seemed he also couldn't say it, at least not in front of me. He coughed into his hand.

Surprisingly, it was Kaem who put her hand on my arm and said, "Estrid rides the stars with her ancestors now." It was the perfect Ahvoli turn of phrase, what we preferred to say when someone died.

"I'm sorry. She was a strong warrior and a loving sister. We will all miss her." Quynn's expression didn't change, but I knew she meant it. She didn't say things unintentionally.

To keep myself from crying, I had to change the subject. "How did you know to come down?"

She pointed to the pyre. "We saw the fire through the clouds. What happened?"

I turned to Arun pointedly. "Maybe you can take Kaem on board, show her around a bit."

He nodded and guided the girl up the gangplank. I felt relief when they disappeared from view. Then, I told Quynn the whole sordid tale—about the cabin and Savarah and the dead priests and the dead girl who might or might not have been the heir, and about finding Kaem who also might or might not have been the heir.

"Where is Stiarna?" Renwick asked. He and the griffin had bonded after she rescued him after the air battle.

I wrung my hands together. "She's gone. She went over a waterfall fighting a manticore."

The sailor's face fell with disappointment, and I realized for the first time that he held a parchment-wrapped dead fish in his hands.

"I'm sorry," I said.

He shook his head. "No, I'm sorry. You lost so much."

Quynn held up a hand, a ruby-red gem glinting on her middle finger. "We all have. The question, though, is what now?"

"Kaem has to get to either Lunla or Ravyn. That's where the sisters were trying to take her when they were killed."

"I can do that," Quynn agreed. "Let's go."

I put a hand on her sleeve before she could turn away. "I'm not going."

She paused, half-turned. "What will you do?"

"If she really is the heir, I promised Ravyn that I would help her, but she and I can't be together. It's too dangerous. The only way I can help her is by continuing to be the Suun heir." I would stay here, lure the ur'gels and Savarah away from the ship. It was the least I could do. I wasn't really the heir. I couldn't close the prison. And I couldn't train the heir, not without risking her life. But what I could do was take out one of Dag'draath's generals. I had a bone to pick with Savarah. She owed me her life, and I was going to take it, even if it cost me mine in exchange.

"Does Arun know?"

I let go of her sleeve that had been pinched between my fingers. "No. I don't— I think he should go. I think Kaem will need him."

Quynn nodded. "I agree. If she doesn't have you or Estrid, he'd be the next best thing."

I cringed at the effortless way she said my sister's name. Would I ever be able to do that, think of her without it hurting?

"Sorry," she said again.

"It's fine." I shook my head. "Or it will be. I'm glad … I'm glad that others will remember her, you know?"

"I will," Quynn promised, sounding kinder and more sincere than I'd ever heard her before.

"You should go, before Arun gets back."

The ship was still at full sail, and it was only a matter of minutes before the gangplank was raised and the *Wind Wraith* took to the air. It rose too slowly, though, and when it was only a few yards up, Arun's face appeared over the edge. I should have walked away, turned my back on him and sent him a clear message, but I was frozen. Kaem was beside him, her innocent face contorted with confusion.

"What are you doing?" I heard Arun shout to Quynn.

I didn't hear her reply, but Arun disappeared and then reappeared, further away with each moment. I willed him to calm down, to see reason and stay on board, to leave me to my real destiny, the one that I controlled, not the one thrust upon me.

Of course, he wouldn't cooperate. He went to the bow of the ship and climbed onto the railing.

"Arun, no!" I shouted up to him. "Don't be stupid."

"You promised," he yelled back.

I had no comeback for that. It was true that I'd promised to take him with me wherever I went. That I wouldn't leave him behind. But couldn't he see that he was the one doing the leaving? It would be better this way. He would be safer, and he would be able to keep Kaem safe, no matter who she was. It was what he was good at. I was death personified; he was life.

Maybe not for long, though.

He stepped off the railing, one of his wrists wrapped in a rigging rope.

I gasped but didn't cry out, not wanting to distract him from whatever his idiotic plan was.

The rope swung him in a wide arc until he smacked against the hull, grabbing the empty hull net, and releasing the rope. The wide-eyed sailors above reeled it in. He shimmied down until he was at the bottom, as close to the ground as he could get, though it was still very far up, and then let go.

His fall somehow lasted both a split second and an eternity. He was on the ground and the *Wind Wraith* was disappearing into the clouds in the blink of an eye. When I reached him, he was immobile on the ground, a heap of limbs.

"Arun." I rolled him to his back only to find him staring up at me, grinning. "Asshole."

He winced when my fist connected with his chest. "Ow."

"Serves you right. What were you thinking?"

He tugged me down on top of him and I let him. "That elves live very long lives, and I didn't want to spend a single moment of it without this." He pressed his mouth to mine, squeezing me tight around the middle as if still afraid I would run away and leave him here.

I shifted and he grunted. "What is it?" I asked against his mouth.

"Pain," he groaned. "I mean, I jumped out of an airship for you."

"Come on." I stood and held a hand out to him.

He stood slowly, like an old man first thing in the morning, stretching his back and grunting. "Where are we going?"

"To kill Savarah."

"Where will we find her?"

"We won't have to." I smiled and turned east, heading back to the cabin. It seemed appropriate that this place which had been a safe haven for the Suun heir for so long would be her final resting place. "She's going to find us."

CHAPTER 24

The cabin was a welcome respite after days in the open, always sleeping with one eye open and watching for threats stalking us through the grasses. It was just as we'd left it, our footprints undisturbed.

"We should rig some traps and alarms," Arun suggested as we crossed into the garden, the gate creaking. "Especially if we can't draw our weapons inside the protection zone."

I thought it was a good idea. Though the protection spell had weakened, it was still strong around the house, fed, I thought, by the priest's sacrifice. Her blood soaked the ground and kept this place safe. If Kaem and her sisters had never left, maybe their story would have had a different ending, and so would Estrid's. But they'd been afraid, hunted. I couldn't blame them, not really.

While Arun set to work sharpening the fence posts into stakes, I scoured the house for anything I could find—wire and hooks that had been used for fishing, tin cups and an iron bell, spring-loaded mouse traps that had never been used. A cabinet full of potions and powders revealed a jar labeled "galestone" which I gleefully grabbed, giving a little squeal of excitement.

When I came back outside, Arun had already dug a couple of

holes at the garden's entrance and set the stakes upright inside of them, then covered them with straw. I helped him rig a couple of tripwires using the wire and tin cups, and we set up a few more spear traps around the house.

"I never thought I'd be using hunting snare traps to kill ur'gels," I said offhandedly as I tied off a hair trigger that held back one of the stakes.

Arun touched the wire, testing its tautness. "I never thought I'd even see an ur'gel in real life. They're just storybook monsters from my childhood."

It was nearly dark by the time we finished, and thunder rolled overhead, the dark grey clouds blocking out any light from the moons or the stars. I would have felt better if I had been able to search the stars for Estrid. If I could feel like she was watching over me.

Instead, I went inside with Arun and we built a small fire in the hearth and warmed up a portion of stew we'd found stored in the icebox. It was good and warmed our bellies. The rain began to fall, the drops loud on the thatched roof, making conversation pointless.

Arun went to bed while I stayed up, whittling a few more stakes out of spare posts that had been stacked against one wall. I felt restless, afraid to sleep because of what might come to me in my dreams, and because of what I might wake up to. Savarah's cruel smile. An ur'gel's hand around my throat. The end of my world.

Thunder crashed and I jumped to my feet, the ground shaking. I padded on bare feet to the bed at the back of the house, climbing under the furs beside Arun. He grunted and shifted, rolling automatically to the side so I could fit myself in against him.

Instead of closing my eyes, I stared at him until he blinked back at me, roused from sleep by the sheer force of my will. Without saying anything, I tipped my head up and kissed him.

He didn't miss a beat. His arm tightened around me, while his free hand slipped under my shirt, exploring the hard lines of muscles and the subtle curves of my hips and breasts. I pressed myself against him, wanting more. If this was to be the end, our last normal night, then I wanted all of him.

He rolled, pinning me beneath him. I closed my eyes, focusing on the solid weight of him on top of me, pressing me into the thin mattress, grounding me in the here and now. I wanted to lose myself in the moment. To let his wandering kisses erase the stain of grief and the fear of what the next day, or the day after, might bring.

As if he could feel the direction of my thoughts, he tried to pull away, but I fastened myself securely around him, my teeth grazing his shoulder threateningly. He chuckled, a deep, throaty growl that reverberated between us, and dropped his face to my neck, tracing kisses steadily and deliciously downward.

Sometime later, we lay in a sweaty pile of limbs. Outside, the storm had tapered off into a pleasant shower that tried desperately to lull me to sleep. The furs had fallen to the floor, but neither of us moved to retrieve them. His breathing grew steady and deep, and I thought he'd fallen asleep until I felt a callused thumb forming lazy circles on my palm. I looked over at him from where I lay in the crook of his shoulder.

"Hi," he said, his voice deep and rough.

"I don't hate you," I whispered, knowing I should have said that earlier.

"I know."

"And I don't hate what we did."

He cleared his throat. "I don't either."

Sleep came easily after that, in spite of the looming threat, and when I closed my eyes, it was Estrid's smiling face that appeared behind my eyelids.

I woke up tucked against Arun, his body curved around mine. The sound of a bird chirping beyond the window signaled it was morning, and that the rain had stopped. I realized this was what it would be like to be *normal*. To fall in love, to share a home, to wake up beside each other every morning with nothing ahead of us except our daily chores and finding excuses to sneak off together, just the two of us. We could buy a plot of land outside of Bor'sur, within walking distance from my father's home.

But that was just a useless dream. It would never be our reality.

When I made a move to sit, Arun pulled me back against him, nuzzling his face into my neck.

"We should get up."

"Yup," he said sleepily.

"I have to get dressed."

"Nope."

I pushed him away and he fell back, laughing. It was such a common sound, but one I wanted to commit to memory.

As we dressed, he talked about the cabin and how we could fix it up, the slight changes we could make to make it more livable. How easy it would be to replenish the garden. I realized he was stuck in that same in-between place where I'd been when I woke up that morning.

I had just finished buckling on my leather vest when there was the faint sound of jingling bells.

I froze. "Shhh," I insisted.

Arun looked up at me mid-sentence, his hands on his boot laces. "What is it?"

It could have been the wind, or an animal disturbing the trip wire. But I didn't think it was. Even with the necklace on, I could feel her. "Someone's here."

He raised his eyebrows. "That was quick."

We made our way to the front of the house and tugged a curtain aside, peering out through the small window by the door. It was Savarah, flanked by three ur'gels. All three of them had black, leathery wings tucked behind their backs, the tips poking over their heads. While they had a humanoid look to them, they had the blue-tinted skin of their race, and two of them had abnormally long limbs, like ponies standing on their hind legs. The third was larger, standing several feet taller than Savarah, and barrel-chested. The four of them surveyed the cabin and the yard, looking reluctant to come any closer.

Arun let the curtain fall closed. "What do we do?"

"This is why I didn't want you to come."

"What are you talking about?"

I steeled myself, turning to face him. "I'm going to kill her, no matter the cost."

"I know, that's what—"

"Even if it costs me my life. She must die for what she did to my sister. Before she can do that to anyone else I love. I will die to save them. To save you." As soon as I said the words, I realized what they meant. I was finally willing to die for my own lost cause.

Before Arun could respond, Savarah's voice interrupted us. "Frida Suun? Are you in there? Won't you come out to play?"

I wasn't going to slink around and try to escape. I was ready for this. Ready to meet her head-on.

I opened the door. "Savarah. How good of you to join us."

Her smile was dazzling. "I think maybe we've gotten off on the wrong foot."

"You think? You think turning my siblings against me and poisoning my friend was the wrong foot? I have to agree."

Her blue gaze flicked to Arun. "Good job finding that cure, by the way. Only you." She shook her head as if impressed.

"I wouldn't have let you take him. How did you think you would win me that way? By hurting the ones I love?"

"Perhaps I went about things all wrong. But you have to understand, when I heard about the girl with the star beside her eye and Onen Suun's blood in her veins, I had to find you.

But I had just escaped from the prison. The slavers picked me up and turned me over to the elves on Fairlow. Laurel Trisfina was putty in my hands, and his daughter was even easier to manipulate. Her bleeding heart was my ticket to Barepost. To you."

It had never been about Arun at all. He'd only been a happy accident. "But you left."

"I never expected to see Beru." She laughed. "The only other person outside of the Barren Wastes who could recognize me, and I run into him on a Bruhier cliff. Foregin has a twisted sense of humor, I'll give him that." She spoke as if she knew the god of fate, and for all I knew, maybe she did.

"Why didn't you just kill me and get it over with?"

The ur'gels beside her were getting restless. Savarah held up a hand and they went still. "Oh, no, Frida darling. You are far too powerful, no, too pivotal, to waste in death. You have a choice to make, and that choice will affect the rest of the world."

"Light or dark." I spoke in a low voice, but she still heard me.

"That's right. Choose the light and I'll make everyone you love suffer, and I'll make you watch until you're begging me to end it for you."

"What if I choose the dark?"

Her lips twisted together before she answered. "Did you know I felt your rage? I heard you calling to me. I almost came. Not to kill you, but to convince you to use your rage to set the world on fire. Use it to free Dag'draath, not imprison him."

I shook my head. "I would never choose the dark. You and I will never be on the same side. Nothing you say will convince me."

"Shame." With a flick of her fingers, she waved the ur'gels forward. "Get the elf. Leave the girl for me."

One of the smaller ur'gels stepped forward and fell, his leg disappearing into one of Arun's spear traps. He screamed and jerked his leg out. It was covered in black blood.

Savarah looked down at him with disdain. "Carefully," she said, raising an eyebrow, unaffected by his screams.

An arrow whistled past my ear and buried itself in the ur'gel's temple, putting an end to the screaming. He toppled sideways. I turned to Arun with wide eyes.

He shrugged, his bow in his hand. "I don't think the protection spell applies inside the house."

Well, that was a game changer. I pulled my ax and sword to test Arun's theory and wasn't zapped into unconsciousness.

The other two ur'gels advanced into the yard.

"I've got this," Arun said, stepping around me and leaving the safety of the house. "You get Savarah." Then, to the ur'gels, he crooked a finger. "Come on, boys."

Savarah waited for them to pass through the yard before advancing herself, her eyes on me and on the ground in front of her. I knew she wasn't one for hand-to-hand combat, but she didn't have much of a choice here. She couldn't use her powers against me because of the locket, and she couldn't draw a weapon outside of the house.

There was a crash beside me, and I turned to see the other smaller ur'gel caught in one of Arun's traps. That moment of distraction was all Savarah needed. She dove, tackling me back into the house, knocking my weapons from my hands.

She straddled my hips and drew two small knives that she slashed at my face. I bucked my hips to try to get her off, but she was immovable. Her knives left dozens of small, stinging cuts on my arms and hands as I fended her off. I wasn't able to get my feet under me or my hands on my own weapons. Instead, I reached up and pressed my thumbs into her eyes with a growl.

She howled and grabbed for my wrists, and then finally rolled off me when I didn't let go.

My fingers scrambled against the wooden slats of the floor and closed around the hilt of my sword. As Savarah rolled to me, her knives raised, I plunged the sword into her chest, shoving with both hands.

I never forgot what it felt like to kill another person. It was always the same. It wasn't like slicing through a strip of beef. The body resisted, bones and muscles holding on until finally, under an intense and unexpected show of force, they snapped and broke and died. Savarah might have been immortal, but she was still human.

Savarah's eyes went wide, the blue pools tearing up as she stumbled back, taking my sword with her. Her hands wrapped around the hilt of the sword, which was right against her chest. Her mouth dropped open in surprise when she looked down at it.

But when she looked back up at me, her look of surprise morphed into one of amusement.

She wasn't falling over dead.

She was pulling the sword out of her chest, but blood wasn't pouring down her dress and pooling on the floor. She flipped it back and forth in front of her, examining the blade which was painted red with her blood. I was the one with the look of surprise on my face now, and she laughed when she saw it.

"You can't kill me that way, little bird."

And then she brought the hilt of the sword down against the side of my head with more strength than I knew she had.

I slid to the ground, fighting unconsciousness.

She knelt and touched two fingers to my throbbing forehead. "My parting gift, dear Suun. Until we meet again."

The last thing I saw were her slippered feet walking away before the world went black.

CHAPTER 25

I took a deep breath and when I exhaled, my breath was a white cloud in the cool air. The rabbit hung from a branch just ahead of me, his paw ensnared in one of my traps. I freed it, slit its throat, and hung it from my belt with the others. I wove through the woods, following a well-worn trail, and emerged in a clearing where a two-story cabin sat in the middle of a tended yard, smoke pouring out of the chimney. Home, I knew, even though another part of my brain knew I had never seen the place before. Every part of me, though, recognized that a warm hearth waited for me, and I picked up my pace.

A woman who was kneeling over a raised garden box stood when I reached the gate and turned to me, brushing her yellow hair back over one shoulder.

"Frida," Estrid said, "you brought dinner. I was just picking the vegetables for the stew." She had a basket balanced on her hip, full of carrots, onions, and celery.

My mouth opened, but no sound came out as my mind warred with itself. She was gone, dead and burned, but here she was, standing in front of me. I reached out and touched her cheek.

She laughed and grabbed my hand, shoving it away gently. "What's wrong with you?"

There was a noise behind me, and I turned to find Erik emerging from the woods, his arm around Aysche, whose belly was swollen with child. Another child was hiding behind her skirts, a miniature version of Erik peering out at me with big eyes.

Seeing me staring, he held up a brown paper bag. "I brought the wine." He shoved the wine into my hands and took the strap of rabbits from me. "I'll get these ready while you three catch up." He cut through the garden toward an outbuilding behind the house to clean them.

Aysche stopped to hug me, her bony arms strange around my shoulders.

"Mama." The little boy tugged on her skirts.

She knelt and turned to him. "Yes?"

"Mama, I'm bored."

She smiled indulgently at her son and stood, turning to me and, strangely enough, putting a hand on my abdomen. "Don't worry, it won't be long before you have another little one to play with."

Mouth agape, I looked down at myself and saw the gentle roundness to my otherwise flat stomach.

"Let's go inside," Aysche said, grabbing my hand. "You shouldn't be out here too long in the cold. I can't believe he still lets you hunt."

He? He who?

But I knew.

I knew before the door opened and revealed two men sitting at a dining table with a game of cards between them. One of them was an older man with grey hair and a long beard—my father. The other ... he was softer, his face a little rounder and his hair a little shorter. He didn't wear any weapons when he stood and crossed the room to greet me, arms outstretched.

"Wife." Arun kissed my cheek, and then crouched to put his hands on either side of my belly. "Daughter." He kissed the small bump.

I tugged him back up to standing by the shoulders and held him in front of me, staring. This was the strangest thing of all—Arun and me, settling down, running a home, starting a family. Stranger than my dead sister picking vegetables in the garden, stranger than my brother marrying my former arch-enemy. I kissed him, long and hard, not caring who was watching. I heard the hoots and hollers from our spectators, but I didn't care.

He pulled away, laughing, and patting me on the head. "Later, wife, later. What's for dinner?"

After dinner, which had been a loud, happy ordeal, I stepped outside to get some air. I followed the fence to the back of the house and found myself looking down at the lights of Bor'sur.

I was home.

We were home.

A hand grabbed mine and I expected it to be Arun, come to continue our earlier kiss. I turned, a smile ready on my lips, and instead came face-to-face with cold blue eyes from my nightmare.

But I didn't scream or pull away or reach for my weapons.

She came to stand beside me, her small fingers intertwined in mine. "Isn't it beautiful?" she asked, looking out at Bor'sur.

I was ready to agree with her, but when I turned my eyes back on my town, it wasn't as it had been before. Instead, flames licked the sky, black smoke pouring out of homes and businesses. People ran through the streets, leaving trails of smoke and blood and screams.

Bor'sur was burning.

The world was on fire.

And it was all my fault.

I JERKED AWAKE WITH A GASP, coughing and gagging, trying to get the smell of smoke out of my nostrils. I stood on shaking legs and stumbled to the door, swinging it open. My throbbing head was made worse by the light of a beautiful day.

Arun was facedown on the ground a few feet from the door,

a trail of blood behind him as if he'd dragged himself there. He was quiet and still, unmoving.

I'll make everyone you love suffer, she'd said.

No. No, no, no, no, no.

Not Arun.

I knew it would happen.

I tried to get him to leave, and he wouldn't.

He had to stay, and now he was…

Stupid, stupid elf.

Stupid boy.

I dropped down beside him and rolled him over, my hands and arms trembling. He flopped lifelessly onto his back. There was a huge gash across his chest, from shoulder to hip. But when I put my ear to his chest, I could hear it. The gurgle of strangled breathing and the faint pulsing of his heart.

He was alive. We both were.

I dragged him into the house and slammed the door, then used a knife to tear his shirt away from the wound. There were clean white cloths in the kitchen, and I dipped them in alcohol to clean the wounds. It was a gruesome task, the skin loose and ragged, but when the blood had been cleaned, it looked at least a little better. I found the extra wire and hooks that we didn't use in the traps and sterilized them in the hearth fire before threading them. Taking a deep breath to steady my hand, I forced the needle through one side of the wound, then the other, and pulled, lacing the skin back together.

Over and over I did this, and all the while, Arun didn't stir. I paused every few stitches and listened for the sound of his breathing. Though light, it grew increasingly steady as the bleeding slowed to a trickle. With the last stitch at his hip, he gave a shudder and a low moan.

"Don't move," I whispered, not sure he could even hear me.

I sat back and studied my bloody hands. Estrid was dead.

Erik was gone. There would be no babies, no family dinners. The dream had been just that—a dream. This was my reality. A life of pain and blood, a life where everyone I knew would die just because of their association with me. Savarah would hunt me for the rest of my life and do everything in her power to convince me to free Dag'draath.

But it was better me than Kaem. What would she do with Kaem, who didn't have anyone? Maybe that wasn't the right question. Maybe the right question was: How much easier would Kaem be to turn because she didn't have anyone holding her to the light?

Savarah could never learn the truth: that she was hunting the wrong woman. It was up to me to stay out of her reach, to keep her distracted and on the wrong trail, so that Ravyn and Lunla could do what they had to do with Kaem.

And with Savarah on my tail, it would give me more than enough opportunities to end her once and for all. I would find a way, because Savarah couldn't get her hands on Kaem. The world needed a Suun heir, and it wasn't me.

Kaem was their best chance.

Their only choice.

I just hoped she was the right one.

Continue reading this series, Legends of the Fallen with book 7, Soul Goblet

Grab the free prequel to the Legends of the Fallen series, Falling Suun here:
https://books2read.com/u/3R1ElD

Like the series Facebook page to stay up to date on all new
releases
https://www.facebook.com/LegendsoftheFallen

ABOUT THE AUTHOR

J.A. Culican is a USA Today Bestselling author of the middle grade fantasy series Keeper of Dragons. Her first novel in the fictional series catapulted a trajectory of titles and awards, including top selling author on the USA Today bestsellers list and Amazon, and a rightfully earned spot as an international best seller. Additional accolades include Best Fantasy Book of 2016, Runner-up in Reality Bites Book Awards, and 1st place for Best Coming of Age Book from the Indie Book Awards.

J.A. Culican holds a master's degree in Special Education from Niagara University, in which she has been teaching special education for over 13 years. She is also the president of the autism awareness non-profit Puzzle Peace United. J.A. Culican resides in Southern New Jersey with her husband and four young children.

For more information about J.A. Culican, visit her website at: www.jaculican.com.

ABOUT THE AUTHOR

Cassidy studied English and Creative Writing at the University of North Carolina at Chapel Hill and won the Bill Hooks Award for Young Adult Fiction in 2007. She lives in beautiful North Carolina with her husband, two kids, two dogs, and one cat who thinks he's a dog.

For more information about Cassidy Taylor, visit her website at: http://cassidytaylor.net/

ACKNOWLEDGMENTS

Editor: Frankie Blooding
Cover Artist: Christian Bentulan
Formatting: Dragon Realm Press